W9-AEP-784

# SUGARLAND

Paul Foreman

Thorp Springs Press

*For James and Rose*

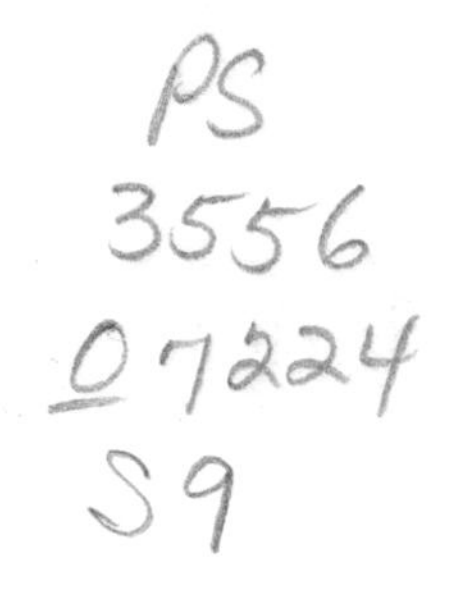

**Illustrated by Andrew Curry**



**Library of Congress Cataloging in Publication Data**

Foreman, Paul, 1943–
Sugarland.

I. Title
PZ4.F7176Su [PS3556.07224] 813'.5'4 77-25171
ISBN 0-914476-76-9

**Thorp Springs Press**
2311C Woolsey St.
Berkeley, CA 94705

ISBN: 0-914476-76-9

## Chapter I PECANS

*"Some rob you with a six-gun,*
*some with a fountain pen."*

Under high limestone bluffs, remnants of the caprock, the Brazos river winds slowly down the length of Texas. From the salt flats on the panhandle it trammels and sifts its burden of soil and fish some thousand miles till it empties at its mouth into the Gulf of Mexico near Freeport. Along the banks tall cottonwoods rear their heads above the pale green willows and the dense glade of the pecan trees.

Texas, like a chameleon, takes on the hue of its surrounding colors. Near Louisiana, Texas resembles Louisiana; the same holds true with New Mexico, Oklahoma, and Old Mexico. Only in the heartland along the long snaky rivers totally within the state: the Brazos, the Colorado, and the Trinity, is Texas uniquely itself both in the land and the people sprung from the land. Sugarland sits on the Brazos.

* * *

Daryl Barnes sat in the Longhorn Cafe that cold December night sipping his cup of coffee to make it last; refills were a nickel a cup. Three weeks now since he had been laid off by the Buckley Ranch after the price of cattle had hit rock-bottom and Old Lady Buckley decided to pinch a few pennies by laying off some of the hired hands. The foreman, Jim Sears, had fought to keep Daryl on, but Miz Buckley, perhaps angered by Daryl's refusal to bow and scrape whenever she passed by in her black limousine, insisted on his dismissal. Daryl remembered, now, in the back of his mind how other hands would pause to tip their hats at the dust of her Cadillac whereas he, out of some pride of race unknown to the others, would go on about his business twisting fence or punching cows.

Wasn't much of a job, anyway. Ten hours a day for two hundred bucks a month pay. Hell, grocery clerks in Fort Worth make more than that. Daryl ran his finger across his forehead along the sweatband of his battered straw hat. He knew that if he didn't get some money soon, it would be Katy-bar-the-door. Sometimes Daryl would contemplate the economy of this forlorn town of Danville and wonder how anybody stayed alive. The people who had the money and land were few, and it baffled him how everybody else managed to live off the crumbs from their table.

He was lost in his musings, pondering how all these people came to be on this particular patch of earth at this time, and how there was nothing, nothing that seemed to hold them all together, when Billy Joe Cresson walked in the door. Billy Joe had been looking for Daryl, simply to talk over hard times. Billy Joe's father, like Daryl's, was almost plumb broke, and he too was out of work.

The Longhorn wasn't much as cafes go. It had the look of ten thousand other short-order stands on the highway across the country, but inside it was different. It had taken on the look of the hard-bitten men who frequented it, mostly cowhands, farmers and river-bottom men, men who did little but hunt and fish for a living. There was more dust on the floor; the leather and oak furnishings were worn down; and the pair of long-horns, the totem of Texas legend now past, spoke a bit more eloquently with their droop and lack of shine.

Billy Joe sat down across from Daryl, a wry grin splitting his face. "Well, have you found a job yet?"

"Nope, nobody's hiring. They're all saving their nickels to scrub their ass with."

"Same here. I went down to the gravel-washer today, and they said they wouldn't be hauling any more gravel until after the spring rains, and then only if the house-building in Fort Worth picked up. So I told them I would be back in May if I was still alive and kicking."

"So all you got for your troubles was a little sand in your shoes."

"Yeah, and it's still sticking in my craw."

"Well, about the same thing happened to me when I went to the strawboss on the Windhoven ranch. I says, 'Ya lookin' for hands?' He says, 'not specially. What can you do?' I says, 'I can mend fence, cut post oak, carpentry, and tend cattle.' Then he says, with a little smirk on his face, 'We've got a feller to do all that,' and so, just like the guy in the Bible, I went away sorrowful."

"Ha! Ha! Ha! We have sure hit upon some busted luck. So, what do you propose we do?"

"First off, have you got a quarter for the jukebox?"

"Sure, but I wasn't planning on spending it that way. What do you want to hear?"

"Whatever. Something with the blues."

He put in the quarter, punched some buttons, and directly, after the whirring and click of the machine, out came the voice of a sad-throated Texas gal singing a mournful, lonesome song.

When Billy Joe sat back down he looked hard straight into Daryl's eyes. Daryl could almost feel his palms sweat knowing that Billy Joe had something on his mind. Finally he spoke. "Daryl, I know where we can get some pecans."

"Huh! You're crazy. Every orchard this side of San Saba has done been gathered either by white folk or wetbacks or coons and possums."

"Well, I know some that the Meskins ain't got. They are sittin' already sacked up down in Kuykendall's warehouse."

Daryl tried to hide his rising excitement. Outwardly he was calm and his voice slow and easy. Some people, usually strangers, mistook his steadiness for timidity, and having riled him, which wasn't easy, would rather have broken into a den of rattlesnakes. He had picked up the nickname of "fearless" when he once rode a jackass which nobody else could sit; he rode it until it stopped bucking and just stood quivering, wringing wet with sweat, then he hopped off (his own knees nearly buckling) and dismissed the jack with a shrug. "He'd be right comfortable if it weren't for that bony backbone." For a long time after that those country boys would tell about "Fearless," and how that unridable jackdonkey had been rode hard and put away wet.

"Kuykendall. Hmmh! I reckon he could afford for a couple of river rats like us to swipe a sack or two of his pecans."

"He'll never know it's gone. We'll do it like Ben Milam sneaking in to San Antonio in the dead of the night. Them meskins never knew what hit 'em."

"Well, if we're gonna turn to a life of crime to stay alive, we oughta rope in Skeet and Danny Smitson. They are dead broke just like us, and their pickup would be ideal for hauling our loot down to Tarrant to sell."

"Good idea. Let's go get them." They got up from the table abruptly, leaving their coffee cups half full. The waitress, Faye, raised an eyebrow, and drawled quietly, "Y'all come back." Daryl, unable to resist an ironic joke, spoke back, "Sure we will, Faye, soon as it starts raining." She blushed and smiled to cover her blush. The two walked on out into the night.

"Ha! Ha! You rascal. You sure would like to get into her britches, wouldn't you?"

"Yeah, if she would pay me, and would lie right still, and wouldn't yelp when it went in."

Driving over to the Smitsons' farmhouse, Daryl and Billy Joe kept cracking jokes, and sat on edge, half out of elation at doing something sneaky, and half shivering while waiting for the heater in the '52 Oldsmobile to warm up.

After a short drive they pulled off onto the dirt road leading to the Smitson place. It wasn't much of a place, just one layer of pine boards, covered over with black tar paper to keep the wind out. Old man Smitson was just a sharecropper and would never live any better. He did not even care to use the wood outhouse he built for his wife and kids, but did his daily job out in the bushes next to the house like a wild animal. Daryl always thought he was more natural in this respect as well as others.

When they drove up into the yard, scattering a dozen Bantam chickens (the reason so many poor people in Texas and the rest of the South keep Banties is one: they're prettier, and two: they just like those peewee eggs better; 'you can't get them like that in the store!'), they blinked the headlights on and off to let the two eldest Smitson boys know they were coming.

Sure enough, Danny and Skeet Smitson came right out the door, leaving a stream of yellow electric light behind them. When only a few people come to see you, you can generally tell who's coming by the sound of the car's engine.

Danny spoke first, "Y'all too late for supper. We done ateup all the pinto beans."

Billy Joe cracked back, "Well, we can wring a few of these chicken necks and throw them in the pot."

Skeeter, knowing his roosters and hens well, said, "If you can catch one of them, then she's yours."

So the four boys, almost grown men, trapped between a carefree boyhood of hunting, fishing and raising cain they couldn't go back to, and a ruthless man's world of property and profit that hadn't yet admitted them, sprawled along the running board and fenders of the Smitson's pickup and hatched their plot.

After a half hour Dan went in and told his folks they were going coon hunting on Cecil Fairchild's farm way down the Brazos. His mother spoke, "Don't y'all stay out all night, and don't shoot anybody's cow either, thinkin' it's a deer like you did last time. We got plenty of chicken to eat."

"Don't worry Mom. We'll be back before sunup with a sackful of ringtails, and maybe a few possums to sell to Nigger Nett."

After they left, the woman, gaunt and homely, her careworn hands shifting the knitting needles almost unconsciously, said to her husband, "Those boys are up to something. They left behind that little Walker pup."

"Mebbe they're gonna hunt somethin' beside coon."

"What are you gettin' at? What's your suspicion?"

"Don't know. Just because I say somethin' doesn't mean I know what I said. It strikes me as how if I was in those boys' shoes, I'd be huntin' some other kind of game than coon."

"Go on, you! You and your nasty mind. If those boys go to hell, I'll know who's to blame." She hushed up then, because she would be pleased in secret if her boys were out chasing some girl, and she was piqued at her man's cleverness; she might not have guessed what he was referring to.

## Chapter II WIDOWS AND MOONLIGHT

*"Uncle Eph's got the coon and gone on, and left us looking up the tree."*

Danny coasted his pickup to a halt in the thick shadow of the stonewalled warehouse. A half moon shone intermittently among the deep-breasted cumulus clouds which filled the night sky. Since they were six years old, all of them had played Cowboys and Indians, or Cops and Robbers, or sometimes simply Guns all over the town and knew every rock, sidewalk and fencepost like the palm of their hand. They had already agreed on a plan and as soon as the moon went behind a cloud, they stealthily eased out of the truck and slid like lizards around the corner of the stone wall.

But there are things older than lizards, and movements of time and eye which are beyond any man's reckoning. In a house some fifty feet behind the warehouse, which itself sat on the courthouse square, and facing the sidestreet, lived an old woman named Miz Ben-Sinai. Everyone thought she was Jewish, and perhaps she was; certainly one of her paternal great great grandparents was. She, however, considered herself as English as primroses, and all the relatives she had ever known were Episcopalians. Whenever anyone asked about her name, she smiled with icy sweetness and said, "It's an old English name, too, you know. Oh yes!" There wasn't an Episcopal church in this part of Texas where her father had dragged her fifty years before because he had to be a cattle rancher, and she didn't attend the local Baptist or Church of Christ often, thinking of them all as low-church; so she sat at home, read her books, tended her roses and lilacs, and received her handful of friends for long afternoon teas and serious conversation, and once a year in the summertime took herself down to Galveston to visit her sister and eat some tasty Gulf shrimp and fresh oysters for a change.

She had trouble sleeping at nights. Not that she wasn't healthy. She ate a good diet of stews and fresh fruit and nuts, as well as yogurt topped with strawberries. No, it was true insomnia. At night her mind waked up, flared like a campfire, and did not burn down until three or four in the morning. She slept well, once she got to sleep, way into the day, and everyone knew not to call on her before noon. Because of her strange habits, her closeness, her short-stepped gait, quick eye, and lively mind, she was awesome, like a witch or sorceress to most of the young people in town and many of the old ones as well.

This particular night she sat in her bedroom by the window rocking and thinking, with the moon at times falling on her sleeve. It seemed, she thought, there was a wall between periods of time; she, for instance, had never understood her own mother, neither her fears nor her pleasures; none understood her today. She loved to contrast the sharp picture of that sealed past in her mind with the vivid scenes which fled before her today. Perhaps that is why she liked moonlight best; the aura of its shine gave a special luminosity to objects, as if they partook of the oldness of the moon when they stood in its light. So she sat, the images outside her window flitting between the spaces in her dream, and she rocked.

A shadow filled the corner of her eye and would not go away; her eye snagged on a new object through the glass pane, tugged her out of her reverie; she looked more closely at the shadow against the rock wall. At first when the eye tries to focus at night it does not work so well; naturally roving, it picks up each object in detail, but when stopped, the multitude of things crowding the corner tend to pull the eye out of focus. Only when she narrowed the sweep of her eye to a short span around the shadow, could she make out a young man. Then two, three more young men joined him. Miz Ben-Sinai clutched the arms of her chair, startled and excited by this strange scene outside her window. She at once realized how full the moonlight fell on her, and drew back her chair behind the curtain, and peeked from the corner of her window like a peeping-tom.

The teen-age boys engaged in lightning debate over how best to break into the warehouse; Skeet Smitson held a tire iron and wanted to pry the sliding sheet-metal door back. Billy Joe told everybody, "Just hold your potatoes. You'll make more noise than a den of foxes. I've already spotted the best way to get in." With that, he started to climb the thick Spanish oak which stood up against the wall. He skinned up it like a coon or young bear would with arms and legs wrapped clear around it. The other boys saw the second story window he was making for and hushed up. B. J. swung out on a branch, planted his toes on the window ledge, and hung there a precarious moment between the tree and the wall. Then, sure of himself, he lowered his weight onto the stone ledge and crouched there like a spider against the stone and glass. Miz Ben-Sinai's eyes widened in amazement.

He then slipped the window up; sure enough, nobody ever bothered to latch the second story windows. Danny said, "I'll go next," but Daryl stayed him with a whisper, "wait and see if he opens it from the inside." B. J. crouched, still as a fox, for a minute after he entered the room, until his eyes adjusted to the darkness. He knew the others would wait for him to try to open the back door from the inside. He saw now that he must be in the main office of the pecan and mohair warehouse. There was the big black safe and a huge rolltop desk as well as a cushioned swivel chair. How he craved to twiddle with the combination lock on the safe; how many times had he heard that if you listen hard you can hear the tumblers click into place. So it was just a matter of turning the knob very slow, to hear the click, then alternating the direction of the turn. But B. J. knew the others downstairs were just after pecans, which they believed would never be missed. Nonetheless, he had to look around some on his own, and started opening the drawers of the roll-top desk (with the side of his finger so as not to leave any prints). In the bottom drawer was a cigar box, *Havana Nuggets*, it read over the picture of a buxom señorita. No cigars, but a handful of folding money. B. J. didn't bother to count it, but carefully slid it into his wallet, then stuffed the change into his watchpocket. Then he stole down the stairs into the high-ceilinged warehouse room.

He opened the back door by lifting the door off its sliding rail. The others, when they saw the door shift open in front of them, slipped quickly into the dark inside of the building. Miz Ben-Sinai's jaw worked absently.

After another quick debate over which towsacks of pecans to take, they settled on those furthest from the door and the front of the room. Each decided to take one sack, which ought to have at least a hundred pounds of pecans apiece. The eyes watching the back of the building now saw the boys return through the slit, this time struggling with the sack of nuts. Daryl led the way to the pickup parked in the shadows, and because he was the strongest, hoisted the sacks up and laid them in the bed of the truck.

B. J. returned to the building, lifted the door back on its runners, then crept back out the same window he had entered, pulling it shut behind him. He then reached for the limb and pulled his way along it hand over fist until he reached the tree-trunk and slid down. The pickup had the quietest loud rumble in its life as it started up and rolled away across the gravel road. After they left Miz Ben-Sinai was disturbed more by the stillness than she had been by witnessing the crime. She took off her clothes, put on a nightgown and crawled into her big four-poster bed. But she didn't sleep that night; her hand kept darting to her breast to feel how fast her heart was beating.

The elated boys burst with laughter when the tension broke inside the truck; exclamations punctured the air like beans popping from their shell. They quickly decided to hide out the rest of the night down on Squaw creek, then drive on into Tarrant the next morning to sell the pecans. When they pulled off the side road and parked at the fishing hole on the creek, they built a fire to break the chill, and swapped stories until dawn broke in the east. Each told of their fear and excitement in stealing the pecans. One sack was broken open; Daryl had thought they were papershells from their rattle; and they hulled pecans til their hunger was sated. Some talk was given to hitting the warehouse again after a week or two had elapsed, and mixed with caution about how best to go about it, and whether or not to hit someplace else, they all agreed that they were in it together. Daryl could almost see the old chains slip away, and though he had forebodings, he, too, entered the splendid wickedness of having gotten away clean.

Thus are thieves born: first comes the necessity and after that the joy, of breaking the law; These are the two midwives; the deliverance sought is found.

## Chapter III SQUIRRELS

*"The wise know many things in their blood . . . the vulgar are taught."*

Cy Reynolds eased his pickup to a halt in front of the warehouse at a quarter of eight in the morning. Reluctant to leave the warm cab, he knew how long it took the little butane heater to warm the cavernous rooms of the store. But the fellows would be along to start their domino game soon, and perhaps old man Kuykendall might drift into town early. Cy stepped out onto the curb, lit up a cigarette and glanced across the town square in the stone-cold dawn. Rubbing his arms to keep warm, he waved and hollered at Shorty Fannin over at the Texaco service station. Shorty waved back.

Cy was never given to much reflection; he worked in town because his father had left him money and lots of land, and it was too easy to find wetbacks to work the land. Though he didn't need to work and could have just loafed, he needed a job to get away from his wife; though pretty, she talked a lot and had too many funny ideas and notions in her head. Cy just liked to eat her cooking and plumb her body at night in bed. This morning though, Cy looked out at the old courthouse and scanned the stores which formed the square and thought, "those old boys that built this town built it to last; don't know anybody that can cut stone like that. I reckon this town's more permanent than any of its people."

Cy unlocked the door and stomped on inside. He lit the butane stove and turned up the burners until the blue flames covered the asbestos backing and licked yellow tongues out at the top of the heater. Then he just stood there stomping his booted feet into the floor until his hands warmed. Cy reached in his shirt pocket for another smoke and found he was out. He figured he would just wait and smoke some of Wheelwright's.

After a half hour or so, Henry Wheelwright, Tom Riley, and Buford Green came in to start their dominos. Now dominos is a mysterious game that some men can sit and play all day, then go home and eat supper, then come back and play all night. If a fellow gets good at it his mind learns to work quick, but in certain limited and curious patterns. That is to say, that certain choices or possibilities will never occur to him. Checkers is even more limited; yet there are people who are simply unbeatable at checkers, no matter who goes first. I'm compelled to add that I never saw them do much else besides play checkers. Chess, on the other hand, is a royal game and a different matter.

As usually happened, Reynolds and Riley were losing most of the games to the older men. Cy, consequently, was smoking a lot and talking loud. "Henry, give me some more of that tobacco."

"Rich as you are, you oughta grow your own tobacco."

"Now, Henry, you know that little bald-headed Mormon in Washington ain't gonna give me a tobacco allotment. That just ain't his style."

"Ha! Ha! Naw, but he's giving you a bale of money not to plant nothing at all. So you can buy your tobacco WHOLESALE!"

"He! He! Here you are tanning my hide in dominoes, and you begrudge me a little bit of makin's for my cigarettes. Well, if you boys will tend the store, I'll run over to Shorty's and buy some store-bought."

"Go ahead on. We'll play moon till you get back."

Cy got up and stretched, then went up the stairs to get cigarette money out of the petty cash box; he liked to milk the store every chance he got.

Buford had just told Henry and Tom he would "shoot the moon" when Reynolds stalked back down the stairs, his face twisted like it was screwed on, his mouth open, and his jaw working.

"Cy! What's come over you? You seen a ghost!?"

"God damn, boys! Call the sheriff! I've been robbed!"

While Henry called Sheriff Blake and William Kuykendall, Cy led the other men up and showed them the empty petty cash box and explained how Kuykendall always kept twenty dollars there in case he wanted to go waste it gambling in the pool hall.

When the sheriff arrived along with his one-armed constable, Sam Wiggins, he stood and listened quietly while Cy poured out his story. Then he walked to the back door and said, "you sure this door was shut like this when you came this morning?"

"I'm certain of it." Blake then took the lock and handle of the back doors in his big fists and shook them hard, rattling the sheet iron. Everybody there almost expected to see the tall sliding doors tumble to the floor; when they still stood, the mystery of someone getting in the building unawares gripped them harder.

Bill Kuykendall, holding his side where his truss held up a recent hernia, came strutting in the front door and spoke to Blake, "What's wrong? What have you found out? Who's been stealing from me?"

"Just hold your potatoes Bill. I aim to turn up with what I can. First, I want to ask you some questions. When you locked up last night, how much money was in your petty cash box?"

At this point Kuykendall's mind worked quicker than usual, thinking of his insurance. "Why fifty or sixty dollars, mebbe seventy counting change."

Blake then spoke to all the domino players, "Why don't you boys show me your wallets, I just want to see how much folding money you got." None of them had more than 8 or ten dollars. Buford complained as he put his billfold away, "Why did you do that Sheriff? Do you think I'm a thief?"

"Naw, Buford. I know you aren't. I just wanted to be sure Mr. Kuykendall here, who's been robbed, don't harbor any suspicions of you." Kuykendall, at this time, was looking pretty hard at nearly everybody.

Blake, then, without speaking to anyone, turned on his heel and walked out of the store. Everyone followed like dumb sheep. As Blake walked around on the side street he studied the ground, but the gravel showed no pertinent signs.

Then he came to the corrugated sheet-iron door in the rear. Taking the locked handles together in his huge fists, he shook the door with all his might. Every soul there, but him, truly expected the door to come unhinged. When it held, Blake stepped back a few yards to survey the scene. Turning to Kuykendall, he said, "Clyde, you been robbed sure enough. But right now I can't figger how whoever it was got into your warehouse to rob you. Seems like you keep it locked tight as a drum." Then began a heated discussion of how somebody got past those bolted doors without leaving any more sign than they did. Cy, aware that he was catching plenty of hard looks, even stumbled up with, "Who knows. They might still be inside hiding in a sack of pecans." At this, loud belly laughs split the chill still lingering in that December morning.

Miz Ben-Sinai's wakeful ears had caught the men's voices a few yards outside her house. She swung her feet out of bed and into her furred slippers and creeped to the window to check on the commotion. By now, it was ten men standing there talking. The sight of the sheriff and his one-armed deputy flooded her mind with sharp memories of what she had seen by moonlight during the night. Once decided she was going to talk to the sheriff, she started pulling on dressing gowns and robes to keep warm when she ventured outdoors. When she had on six or seven over her nightclothes, she shuffled on into the kitchen. She poured herself a tall glass of milk, drank it dry, then wiped her mouth on one of the half-dozen cuptowels hanging around her sink.

Sheriff Blake had been thinking about Miz Ben-Sinai, about whether or not she might have seen something. But he knew her habits, that she was never on the streets before 12 noon, and being fond of his own habits, wasn't about to go knocking on her door before then. Still he was sort of glancing over towards her house about as often as he studied the rock-ribbed back of the store. When his eye caught her screen-door swinging open and Miz Ben-Sinai walking out onto her porch, his stomach growled and he started hitching up his pants all the way around his thick trunk. "Boys, help's on the way. Y'all just stand right here, go on speculatin', and let me go talk to the widow there by myself."

Not a man was there but who wanted to be in Blake's shoes at that very moment since they truly expected him to get the revelation from Sinai about what did or did not happen last night. No one had much to say, but all reached reflexively for the pouch of tobacco in their shirt pockets to roll a cigarette while they were thinking of what they would say about the widow to the other men. That is all, except Wiggins, who with only one fist and a stub of an arm swinging along his ribs, always smoked ready-mades.

As the Sheriff approached the widow, he mentally cursed himself for not having paid her a little more attention in the past. He knew she had one of the best minds in town, but nonetheless thought it was always wrapped up in those books of hers that he knew she got from New York on the day she got them because the mailman was always telling him in Kincaid's cafe about all her books, and was consequently a bit shy of her since he was a man of practical affairs and never figured they would have much to say to each other.

She was already out to her picket fence between her rosebushes. "Good morning, Miz Ben-Sinai. I'm pleased to see you this morning."

"Why Sheriff Blake, you've never been to see me. And the way you pass by me on the street without saying a word, my soul, I sometimes think you've vowed not to even speak to me. And here on this cold frosty morning, if all those men weren't standing over there, I'd almost think you came a-courting."

Blake lightly blushed at her remarks. Being properly chastized, he took a moment to collect his wits before he spoke further. He looked down at her steel-gray hair, the proud lifted eyebrows and the faint ironic smile that played about her mouth. Her body beneath her thick robe still had the shape of a woman though it had not held a man for a long time.

Blake cleared his throat. Time was a lizard stalking flies. . . .

"I'll speak a bit more directly, ma'am. Thieves broke into Kuykendall's feedstore last night and robbed him. We're not even certain yet just how they made their entry. I came over here to speak with you 'cause I—uh—had a notion you might have seen something, heard some commotion during the night."

Her brittle, but warm, laugh thawed the air between them. Blake smiled a bit, knowing that this woman had the wit to make a fool of him. "Well, now isn't that some notion? Maybe I did see something; folks tell me I see some strange and sudden things at times. Of course, it all might have been just a dream that came to trouble my sleep."

Blake muttered good-naturedly, "Now, now I don't want to pry into your dreams, Miz Ben-Sinai. I'm just here doing my job. This feller is missing some money, and if you can tell me anything that'd be of help, I'd be much obliged."

"I'm not sure I could tell you anymore than that white-oak tree there, had you a mind to question it."

Blake's large head swiveled around; his eye slid slowly up the trunk of the live-oak and out the limb which hung like a crosstic above the second story win dow. The window looked shut, but hardly shut, the imagination already dimming perception, doubt vanishing before the idea.

"Well now, I thank you ma'am. Judging from that there skinny limb I reckon it was a squirrel and not a possum that climbed up there, huh." The widow laughed delightedly at this, and the men by the feed-store stood in their tracks, their eyes frozen to the sight of the widow and sheriff talking and carrying on.

"Now tell me, ma'am, how many squirrels did scoot up that tree."

"Why, sheriff, only one; but three were on the ground to catch the nuts."

"Ha! Ha! Nuts, you say. But there ain't no nuts or acorns on that tree."—She didn't say nothing, but just looked at him with one eyebrow lifted a bit. Then it dawned on him what they had been after. "Ah, yes. I see—."

Shifting to a more sober tone, the sheriff asked, "You didn't recognize any of those boys, did you ma'am?"

She was mildly troubled by this question. She knew one of the boys by his size and knew that this sheriff and the judge would stand him up in a men's court and send him to prison for what he did. Quickly then, "Why, no Sheriff. The moon was hidden behind the clouds all the time they were out there. I couldn't tell you who they were or describe them to you, except they looked pretty young. I didn't see their car either, but it sounded more like a pickup."

"Thank you Miz Ben-Sinai. That's a lot to go on. It's been a pleasure talkin' to you."

"Why Sheriff, I was only doing as I should. Now that some ice is broken, maybe you will come visit again. I usually serve tea from two to three."

"That would be a pleasure, ma'am. Now if you'll excuse me, I'll get back to my duties. A good day to you."

"Good day." She turned and hurried back into the warmth of her house, pulling her robe tightly about her to hold in the glow of some of the excitement she felt.

Kuykendall had a slack jaw, but it turned to putty and started working when the sheriff laid out the widow's report. "Ben, four boys climbed through that window last night, and not only rifled that cash box but hauled away several sacks of your pecans. Like as not, you'd have never caught on to your missing pecans if they hadn't taken the money to boot. Now get on in there and count the pecan sacks as best you can; the constable here will take the report. I should have those boys corralled sometime today, if they haven't slipped clean out of town."

## Chapter IV ROUNDUP

*"The Sheriff's gonna get you . . .*
*He's gonna take you down"*

The sheriff knew the Smitson boys had a pickup and likely could have done the burglary, so he headed there first. It was almost noon, and the Smitsons, worried a bit about their boys who had been gone all night, were both afraid and relieved when the sheriff drove up in his Hudson. The sheriff looked at the bleak scene before him: the father sitting on a broken chair, his lungs about gone from too much whiskey and tobacco and too many 14 hour days in the fields pushing a plow or trailing a cotton sack; the square hut was covered with black tar paper held together by two-penny nails driven through bottle caps, and no one would ever imagine it could keep the North Wind from knifing through in the winter.

The sheriff stepped out of his big heavy car (which he kept because he had the odd-fangled notion that the sheriff's car should be different from everyone else's, so they could see him a-coming), shut the door quietly, and walked toward the Smitsons, the mother now in the doorway drying her hands on a cup towel.

"Sheriff, you haven't seen my boys have you?"

"Can't say as I have." Deceptively cool, "Is something wrong?"

"Well, they lit out last night coon huntin' I thought, 'n hadn't come back yet."

"Who were they with? I might be able to tell you something."

Smitson had no reason to suspect the sheriff or anyone for that matter. Probably every day that he lived he gave an honest answer to any and every question put to him.

"Why, Daryl and Billy Joe Cresson. You haven't heard about them, have you?"

The sheriff pulled a cigar out of his pocket and took his time biting off the end and lighting it up, taking two matches to light it. He was just about to start talking when the old beaten red pickup rolled into the yard.

"Well, perhaps these boys themselves can tell us where they've been."

Smitson knew then, and not until then, that the sheriff was there to get his boys. The sheriff was already moving toward the pickup, when the father said low and hard, "Blake, they have done nothing.Let them be."

But Blake had already fixed Danny Smitson's eye with the glare of an angry bull. "I know you boys broke into Kuykendall's warehouse last night and stole some pecans. I've got a witness that saw you. Now, confess up to it."

Danny and Skeet, their faces bent by their weight of guilt and rage at being caught, said nothing at first; the only bright spot being they had already hid their share of the money under the floorboard of the pickup.

"Come on boys, I ain't got all day, and I don't aim to spend it standing out here in the cold."

Skeet broke then, tears streaming down his face, "So we did it! So what! We done spent all the money. What do you know about being poor. . . ."

The sheriff was moved by the boy's outburst and spoke more softly, the father having moved to the side of his boys, "There now, take it easy. It's my job to find you out. Both of you are under age so I don't think the judge will be too hard on you. Those other two—Daryl and Billy Joe were with you, weren't they?"—"Yes"—"and they put you up to it, didn't they?"—"Yes, No, we . . ." "well, it will go rough with them. They're 19 and should know better. Mr. Smitson, these boys will have to go with me down to the judge. We won't keep them overnight; they'll be home by suppertime."

"Y'all go along with the sheriff. I'll talk to you when you get home. I trust him; he's given me his word."

Blake had thought nothing of picking up the Smitson boys; that was all in a day's work. Daryl Barnes was another kettle of fish. His father, Rayburn Barnes, was one of, if not *the* toughest, quietest, honest men in the County. Blake picked up Sam Wiggins, gave Wiggins his 4 inch barrelled pistol to carry and strapped on the 6" Colt .38 on his own belt. He also left word with his Mrs. where he'd be.

The Barnes, too, were farmfolk; Rayburn had sharecropped all his life until he went to work in the steel mill during the war; he had been laid up all winter with a slipped disc in his back suffered while pushing two-inch thick sheets of carbonized steel through a dual band-saw. Their house, like the Smitsons, was set off the road on a hill overlooking the countryside under a spread of giant live oaks. One of the oaks had been uprooted by a great windstorm and lay on its side, but with some roots still buried deep had remained evergreen fifteen years; the Barnes boys called it simply "the Big Tree," its trunk measured eight feet across. The morning it had blown down, their pet guinea hen had perched in the great oak laying on its side and potracked until it woke the family.

Blake thought as he drove his big sleek Hudson up the hill and parked on the gravel some twenty yards from the house that the Barnes were like these great oaks, as tough, as rooted, as evergreen. Daryl was the only Barnes boy at home; the two older boys Philip and Don were out roughnecking in western Colorado, and the young one, Alex, who was just 17, had started college on a scholarship out in California.

When the car drove up, Daryl looked out the window. "It's the Sheriff, Dad. I think they've come to see me." Rayburn turned and looked at his son; his eye flashed on Daryl's tense attentiveness at the window, his body poised like a deer's at the first sound of the hounds.

"Wait here in the house, Daryl. The Sheriff knows he has got to talk to me first. Like as not, we won't be needing you. If I do, I'll call."

Rayburn gritted his teeth against the pain, pushed open the screen door, and sauntered out to greet Blake and Wiggins, who by now were out and leaning on the front fenders of the car. Rayburn admired Blake, whom he thought capable in a certain solid way; he had often cut wild bee-trees on Blake's farm and once helped Blake get in his cotton. But he was troubled. He knew Blake had done time in prison himself in the thirties for peddling bootleg whiskey; that Blake had learned a lot, conwise, and that he wouldn't be here unless it was serious.

"Howdy. You gentlemen are just here in time for supper."

"I wish we had time to stay, and give my regards to Mrs. Barnes. We came on business. I'd like to talk to your boy, Daryl."

"Has he done wrong?"

"The Smitson boys say he and Billy Joe Cresson went with them last night, broke into Kuykendall's

Feed Store, and stole four sacks of pecans and about thirty dollars in bills and loose change. They sold the pecans in Tarrant this morning and likely have either spent or hid the money."

Rayburn's mind was racing: Daryl had said he'd been out all night chasing coon, that they had shot six possum and sold them to nigger John for fifty cents apiece. He thought of the nine prime coon hides stretched on the north wall of his house drying in the stiff winter winds. He knew Blake had told the truth. "Well, I'll ask him and see what he did last night. If he has done as you say, he will own up to it."

As Rayburn started towards the house, Wiggins took a step after him. The elder Barnes spoke low and with authority, "You wait right there." Then he went on into the house, but his presence was still being felt at the car.

"Sam, these people are fierce. It won't do to go stepping on what they feel are their rights. I'll be damned if Texas doesn't seem to breed men like that, as tough and single as the old Longhorns."

Inside, Rayburn was curt with Daryl, but gentle. "Son, these men say you stole some pecans. Is it true?"

"Yes, I did it. But I had reasons. You know I had reasons."

"Then this twenty dollars you gave me is not money you had saved up from your sale of furs."

"Most of it is, Dad. If I go to jail, you'll need it for doctor Gus, and for food. Please don't make me give it back." Tears welled in his eyes. The father clasped his son in his arms, and whispered hoarsely, "Son, Son, Son."

Daryl followed his Dad out to the waiting Sheriff. Rayburn was short with Blake. "He said he did it. I know he must go with you now. John Carson and I'll be down to go your bond in the morning, son, so you'll be out until you stand trial. He's in your custody now, sheriff. I trust you will take care of him."

## Chapter V STONE AND STEEL

*"You're in the jailhouse now"*

Daryl listened to the steel door clang shut behind him, hearing the sound for two minutes after it had ceased to ring. Then he sat down on the bench of the holding tank of the Lipan County jailhouse and began to look at the pale thick limestone in the wall of the jail. From the names scratched in the stones, he figured every leading citizen in the town had been in here at one time or another. "Stumpy Riley," "Fats Wyatt," "Ray Blalock," "Judson Craws." One unknown inmate had carved,

*"Though I will not come this way again,*
*I am thankful that here I've been.*
*The hardness of this stone and steel*
*made me think hard about what's real.*
*The love of home, of bed and board,*
*must steer me clear of this crooked road."*

He stretched out on the hardwood bench. How long had he been here? There was no sure sense of time in jail. He knew it was night time, and that was all. After what seemed hours, the sheriff, who lived on the first floor of the jailhouse, returned with two wool blankets. "Here you are, Daryl. They're army issue. They'll keep you warm." He spread one blanket out on the wood bench, lay down on it and pulled both sides around him trapping the end with his feet, then pulled the other blanket the length of his body up to his chin. The warmer he got now, the better, for the night would soon turn cold.

Later, after he had slept by fits and starts, he was woken by a bird call. "What's a whippoorwill doing in town? There it goes again." "Whi—whi—whip-poor-will." He rolled out of his blankets and crossed to the tall rear window where only the two-inch thick slabs of iron barred his way. Down on the ground was Danny Smitson.

"Daryl, I heard they picked you up. They picked us up, too, and let us go. They're gonna get Billy Joe in the morning. I had to sneak out of the house and walk up the creek by Nigger Brown's to get here without being seen. I'm sorry, Daryl. We didn't mean to tell Blake what happened. He already knew, or had guessed everything. Somebody saw us going in."

"Danny, you ain't give back your money, have you?"

"No, it's safe. What about you."

"No. Mine's done been spent on food and doctor bills. I don't think it's likely they will make Doc Gus cough up that money I gave him. Anyway they don't know where it's gone, and I ain't tellin'."

"Good. Here, I brought you some candy bars, a butterfinger and a baby ruth." He pitched them up, and Daryl caught them the first try. "Daryl, what will come of this? What are they gonna do to us?"

"You and Skeet are both under age. They can't do much to you. It might go hard with Billy Joe and me. Remember last year when we were still in school and swiped that case of cokes off that truck up there. Well, Bodecker said he put that on our record. So, I reckon they could send us up if they had a mind to."

"Surely, they won't. You gotta stay here and look after your Dad."

"I don't think they will, but you can't tell. The District Attorney, Sam Chives, is a real bastard, they say."

"Well, I have to be getting back. I wish there was something I could do. Do you want to bust out? I could go get a hacksaw and a rope. You could hide out up the river in those caves on Thompson Mountain."

"Naw, that's okay. My Dad and Johnny Carson will go my bond in the morning. If I was gonna be in this hole a long time, then we'd plan an escape. But not tonight."

"Well, I'll see you soon. I'll get on back to the house." Danny started to fade away into the dark.

"So long. Thanks for the candy bars, you rascal." But he was already gone.

Daryl went back and rolled up in the blankets, but now he couldn't sleep, not for a while. He kept thinking, "So Danny wanted to bust me out of jail, and hide me out up at Thompson Mountain. Better yet, Red Banks. I'm glad they have kept their part of the loot. Somebody has got to see some good out of this."

And when he did sleep, it was to dream. He was not in a jailhouse now; he was in a world of adventure, a world he had known for a long time, a world of Tom Sawyer and Huck Finn, and jailbreaks.

## Chapter VI CUSPIDORS

*"Such furies as we know shall be set upon thee"*

Daryl had played in the courthouse since before he could remember. In the summers when the whole family would walk to town to meet his Dad when he came home from work at the Bomber Plant, he and his brothers played like squirrels up and down the stairs and bannisters, and beneath the tall cottonwoods on the courthouse lawn they played mumblepeg.

He had never had cause to fear or hate the old huge courthouse chiseled out of the same white limestone bluff as was the jail back in the 1880's. Today, as he walked into the high-ceilinged courtroom where Judge Weaver would hear his case, he felt fear. Never before had the details of the courtroom etched themselves so sharply on the retina of his eye. Every three feet along the back of each bench was a brass spittoon or cuspidor. He would not even have known the name cuspidor but for the signs prominent on the walls which read "Five Dollar Fine for Spitting on the Floor. Please use the Cuspidor." He knew all the tobacco-chewing farmers and their wives that dipped snuff called them spittoons. He figured that the courts had Latin names for everything to make it seem different and impressive.

The courtroom covered the whole middle of the second floor of the courthouse, eighty feet deep and a hundred feet wide. On each side of the courthouse twelve windows rose two and a half feet wide, and twelve feet high, with a Spanish arch at the top. The wood paneling on the walls and the upright timbers which held up the roofbeams were all oak. Under the many coats of old varnish, the wood gleamed dark red and heavy.

Billy Joe and his father, Danny and Skeet and their father, were already in the courtroom. Not a single mother had come, as if what was to happen were some ancient ritual to be performed only before men. Daryl later learned that mothers often came to court, but that they never accepted it; they could show their tears and grief to the judge, and the judge be more shamed than they.

Daryl had been taught by his parents never to judge a man until you knew him well, never a snap judgement. But the sight of Sam Chives gave him pause. Sam was a big man, finely dressed in a grey suit and vest, with a heavy gold watchchain draped across his thick waist. His face was florid, pockmarked, and fat; a black cigar jutted six inches from one side of his jaw, and under rimless thick spectacles his eyes continually flashed and shifted. Sam Chives seemed the most evil man Daryl had ever laid eyes on.

Sheriff Blake cleared his throat as the thin wiry man in black robes entered from a vestibule. "This Court is now in session. Will everyone stand for his Honor." Everyone stood. If Chives looked malignant, Judge Weaver was totally the reverse. His short auburn hair was parted in the middle and slicked over to the sides in a quaint manner, with short tufts jutting out above his ears. His clear blue eyes smiled out at the assembly of men and boys and, some would say, positively twinkled with pleasure. Daryl had a flash that the Judge looked like an old photo of Ralph Waldo Emerson he had seen in a book.

"Be seated please. We have only one case to hear this morning, and we will try all four defendants together. I have an afternoon session of this court in Steubenville. Mr. Walters, I understand you have chosen to represent the defendants, who, being indigent, could not afford their own counsel." At this, a thin shallow-faced man in a nondescript blue suit, whom Daryl had not previously noticed, arose to address the judge.

"I do so choose to represent them, your honor."

"You understand that the sum this court can pay you for representing indigent defendants is fixed by law at the sum of $25 per defendant, and understanding that, do you hereby accept that as your fee for such representation."

"Yes, your honor."

"Then I hereby appoint you lawful counsel for all four defendants in the case of the State of Texas against Daryl Robert Barnes, William Joseph Cresson, Daniel Raymond Smitson, and Obadiah Laughlin Smitson sometimes known as 'Skeeter.' " At this, a small ripple of mirth in the court. "Now, how do the defendants plead to the charge that on the night of December 18th, they did each and severally break into Kuykendall's Feed Store in the town of Danville and steal an estimated $75 worth of pecans and a possible other $30 in small bills and loose change, this being a breaking and entering under cover of darkness, a charge of burglary in the first degree, and the theft of more than $50 in farm produce constituting grand larceny."

They plead guilty, your honor."

"Is there any reason why I should not pass sentence upon them this same day."

"No, your honor."

"Be seated. Sheriff, call the defendants. The juveniles first."

Blake rasped out in his gravelly voice, "Daniel Smitson, Obadiah Smitson, rise, come forward and face the bench." The two boys went forward and stood before the judge, since they did not know what bench the sheriff meant.

The judge adopted a kind but stern tone, "Since you two are younger, doubtless your opinions are unformed and you were probably led into this escapade by the older boys. You are under age and the law forbids me from sending you to prison. Furthermore you are both still in school making fair and passing grades. It is not the intention of this court to take you out from under the rule of your parents, though it is apparent from your misdeeds that your parents have been remiss. I hereby suspend sentencing and release you to your father with the stipulation that should you stand convicted before this court again of any offense, misdemeanor or felony, I will then sentence you to one year in the State House of Corrections for Juveniles at Gatesville. I would advise you to be on your best behavior since the Sheriff and his Deputy will be keeping an eye on you. You may be seated. The other two, Sheriff."

"Daryl Barnes and William Cresson, come forward and face the bench."

Daryl knew then the fear he had been feeling. He had run a trapline on Cedar Bluff when he was younger, trapping coons and skunks and selling their furs to make pocket money; once his father had made a water set up on Robinson creek and caught a mink. He knew now that he was like that wild animal caught in a steel trap and lunging to be free. Everything was spinning as he realized the nature of the trap that some god, or devil, or fate had laid for him. He glanced at the livid face of

Chives; Chives was leaning forward from his chair like a fox ready to pounce on a rabbit.

"You boys are men, now, of legal age and fully accountable for all your actions. As your defense counsel acknowledged, you plead guilty to burglary in the first degree in these writs of confession which you signed in the presence of Sheriff Blake. Is there any reason I should not pass judgement now?"

"No."

"No."

"I hereby sentence you both to the minimum prescribed by law of two years at hard labor in the state penitentiary. Mr. Prosecutor, is there any reason why I should not suspend this sentence and substitute three months in the County jail?"

At this, Sam Chives sprang from his seat, dangling the long slobbered cigar in his right hand and gesticulating with his left. "Yes, your honor! Both these fellows have a prior record. True, it's only a misdemeanor record of petty theft. But even petty theft with a prior is a felony, punishable in the state prison. These two have gone and committed a felony on top of the petty theft. It clearly shows a pattern, your honor. They would rather steal than work for a living." There was a faint but distinct scuffling of feet in the court, probably by the elder Barnes. Chives turned his head; something caught his eye and he paled. He turned for his seat, but threw a last word at the judge, "full sentence."

Weaver looked at his hands, his brow wrinkled in thought. It wasn't right sending these boys to prison, but then nothing was right. Chives had never told Weaver to his face that he would run against him in the next election for the district judge's seat, but there were a lot of mutterings to that effect. Chives could bullshit like a prize Aberdeen Angus, and a case like this, if he eased off on the boys, would be the kind of straw

Chives could make into hay. Weaver looked up and glanced to his right at the grim faces of Kuykendall, Reynolds, and the other men from the feed store. He did not look at either Rayburn Barnes or the elder Cresson; he had seen their faces once and did not wish to look again. There's nothing so dispensable as a lenient judge. The solid pen fumbled into his hand. "The sentence stands."

"You will have the possibility for early parole as provided by law, if your behavior in prison warrants it. I now bind you over into the custody of Sheriff Blake and charge him with delivering you both to the state authorities at Huntsville. This court is now adjourned." Weaver's face was stern as he gathered up his papers, handed some to the court clerk, then stalked from the courtroom.

Rayburn was now facing his son, Daryl, across the railing. Blake was at his elbow. "Don't be afraid son. You can bear it. Your mother and I will drive down to see you every other Sunday if we can. We'll get by. I'll take out a loan on the house if need be. Don't worry. We'll try to get you out on parole after six months. God will be with you." Daryl kept choking back his tears as the Law led him away.

## Chapter VII "DRIVE FRIENDLY"

*"and the whole country north of the Rio Grande was named after the Tejas Indians, who were completely friendly to the Spanish padres; their name, Tejas, means 'friendly.' "*

Blake and Wiggins packed Billy Joe and Daryl in the back seat of the big Hudson, handcuffing them together right to left. They pulled away from the old stone jail at seven o'clock in the morning the day after Christmas. The sun bled red in the eastern sky like the sharp cry of a hawk.

Each time Billy Joe and Daryl glanced at one another, grim ironic smiles flashed and went. Though warmly dressed, the chill air still crept through the windows of the car and curled around the boys' pants legs. The heater worked only for the front of the car; Blake and Wiggins were almost cozy as they cracked the latest crude jokes they had heard.

Blake took an obscure highway that stayed west of the Brazos, passing under the shadow of Comanche Peak, then through the small towns of Glen Rose and Valley Mills, crossing such branches of the Brazos as Squaw Creek and the Paluxy River. Daryl knew a more direct route would have been through Godley and

Midlothian, catching the main freeway from Fort Worth heading south; he supposed Blake went this way because he liked the countryside, especially the sharply eroded plateaus that rimmed the basin of the Brazos valley. The Brazos, the oldest and longest river in Texas, with many creeks and smaller rivers running into it—hence its name Brazos de Dios, the Arms of God—flowed from the high plains of the Panhandle above the Caprock down the length of Texas to the Gulf of Mexico.

Texas is very old geologically; earthquakes are unknown as it is the most stable land mass on the North American continent. Daryl recalled his father remarking about the steady earth being one reason Texans had such unbounded confidence in themselves. His own confidence was well-shaken by now; he thought briefly of the prison at Huntsville—what it must be like—with deep foreboding.

Now, he was following the path of the Brazos down into the heart of Texas, in chains. He thought of the Comanches whom the Spaniards captured and enslaved near where he grew up, then led them down much the same path to the silver mines near San Saba. No one knows how much silver those Comanches fished out of the earth for the King of Spain, but it was much. The last pack train to leave the mines, forty burros laden with silver ingots, was overwhelmed by a war party of Comanches with only a handful of the Spaniards escaping to tell the tale. After the turbulence of Mexico's brief war of independence with Spain flared and died down, soldiers were sent once again into Texas to look for the mine; the Comanches had closed the wound in the earth well and sealed the secret among their tribe, thus destroying the grounds for their enslavement, so that the fabled San Saba silver mines became lost, and are lost to this day.

Daryl thought, "At least I won't be that kind of slave. I won't have to dig silver or spend the whole day busting up rock."

As the winter sun rose higher in the sky and collected through the car windows, some of the chill melted away, and the two prisoners relaxed and stretched out their legs. Wiggins, who had turned to dipping snuff from chewing tobacco when he lost his teeth, took off his coat, tapped a teaspoonful of snuff into his lip, and leaned back, laying his stump of an arm along the back of the front seat. Billy Joe stared at the sawed-off arm intently; each time Wiggins moved, he pictured the nerves and tendons working to move the invisible hand and forearm which still clung to the stump.

Daryl kept gazing out the window at the landscape passing by. He hated the billboards and highway signs which interrupted the flow of images. The land was sacred to him, had been sacred to his father, and would be to his sons, if he ever had any. Funny, but true, he felt the fear of a man who knew he might die and never have a son. He had heard stories about prison: how they fed you saltpeter just like in the Army that kept you from ever getting hard and wanting a woman. He'd also heard that many convicts turned queer; he guessed that would be because of the saltpeter, too.

These farmers sure used a lot of tobacco to cut the monotony of plowing and cultivating their fields. The signs read:

DAY'S WORK
Chewing Tobacco
"One chaw will last all day"

W. T. GARRETT SNUFF
"Mild, finely powdered, good nose."
Washington and Jefferson had the habit too.

BLOODHOUND CHEWING TOBACCO
"The best scent for your cents"
Try a plug today!

And there was "BEECHNUT," and "Bull of the Woods," and "Red Tinsley," and "Bull Durham" signs. His father had always chewed "Bloodhound," which came in a thin hard black quid which being impossible to bite through had to be sliced with a pocketknife. Many's the time when picking cotton as a boy, and barefoot, he was stung by a red ant or a bull nettle and his father cooled the pain with a spittle of tobacco juice and the words: "takes a little poison to kill poison." Daryl was of the mind that the finest taste was a sliver of Bloodhound in the mouth when he was in swimming in the river. His Dad had always warned him off of Beechnut by telling him, perhaps in jest, but Daryl believed it, that in the big cities they had men with nails on sticks picking up cigar butts off the streets and that these were later ground up and mixed with molasses to make 'Beechnut.' Daryl knew that people who chewed Beechnut were alcoholics who chewed it mainly for the sugar; he had seen Buck Winters go through a whole package in a couple of hours. The only loose, stringy chewing tobacco he had ever seen his Dad chew was a dry long-cut brand called "Five Fingers" a fellow from Arizona had given him.

The highway signs were as numerous as the billboards, and, seemed to Daryl, just as useless. "Watch for Cattle." Hell, if a driver can't see a cow standing in the middle of the road, it won't do no good to "watch" for it. But the one which to him seemed the most useless, and—if he had known the word—carried the most irony, was a simple inverted triangle that appeared regularly every three miles and read: DRIVE FRIENDLY.

Somehow, while being packed off to prison at the age of 19, Daryl could not imagine Texas friendly. FRIENDLY, in capital letters, was the favorite word Texans had to describe themselves. But, friendly towards whom? Other white men? Daryl knew most Texans surely weren't friendly towards Mexicans or Niggers. And on the plains along the upper Brazos, where the old stories were still told, the last word to describe an Indian would be friendly. Friendly, even then, for only certain other white men. He recalled vividly the Baptist church picnic at which a woman from Illinois was visiting with a young baby. Two teenage girls were dandling the baby on their knees until they learned the mother was from Illinois; the one pitched the baby on the ground, said "Let's don't play with a damned Yankee," and stalked away, leaving the child to squall.

Friendly? Only if you "had money" were other people who "had money" friendly. True for Texas as well as any other place and time. Daryl knew that prison lay at the end of his day's drive; each "Drive Friendly" sign drove a nail through that knowledge.

## Chapter VIII Bois D'Arc, Brahmas, and a Barditch

*"Freedom . . . is a lonely scornful song*
*the wind has taken."*

The sun was way up into the day when Blake stopped the car at a crossroads filling station to gas up. Both men got out of the car, stretched, and dug for nickels in their pockets to get a soft drink. Standing there guzzling on the Soda water, Wiggins had a twinge of remorse about the boys handcuffed in the car. "Sam, reckon it's okay for them to have a Dr. Pepper."

"Sure, won't hurt nothin'. Let them split one between them."

Wiggins poked his head in the car window. "You can have one soda pop between you; all they've got here are Dr. Peppers and Barq's Root Beer. Which will it be?"

"Dr. Pepper" they spoke together. When it came, Daryl took just a few swallows and gave the rest to Billy Joe who swigged it down like a man dying of thirst. Then the sheriff and stubby constable were back in the car and driving.

Deeper into east Texas now, some pines starkly green among the barren elms and Bois D'Arc. The hills were long and rolling, cut by lazy creeks and sloughs.

Here and there the stubble of a cornfield. A lot of cattle, Herefords, Santa Gertrudis, Angus, and a few Brahmas scattered in the herds. Texans were turning a lot to the Brahmas, to crossbreed them with their shorthorns and Mexican stock. Something about the way they could stand the summer heat and that hump in their shoulders, something old and wise in that hump. Even their face was intelligent, almost as quick as a Jersey. Daryl thought of a Black Brahma bull he had seen at a cattle auction the past summer. With long sharp horns that curved straight up over its head, the coal-black bull charged into the auction pen and sent everyone flying up over the fences. No one bid on the bull; no one wanted it, if it could not be fenced. Everyone pitied whoever was trying to sell it. Daryl was so fascinated by the tall lean bull, its beauty, that he climbed around in the pens until he found it. Truly wild, the bull stood still and looked steadily at Daryl, spooking him. Riding in the car now, going down to prison, Daryl remembered his wish about that black Brahma bull. He had wanted it to be free.

Billy Joe, who knew the road and the country, suddenly spoke, "Mr. Blake, I've got to take a leak awful bad. Could you stop, please sir."

"You should have went back yonder at that service station. Wiggins, why'd you buy them that soda water? Well it's another sixty miles to Huntsville; I reckon we can stop."

When they had pulled over and unloaded the boys still cuffed together out of the car, Blake took and changed the cuffs, cuffing them right to right. In case they took off running, he knew they could not get far in such an awkward fashion. "Okay, you can walk down into the barditch, out of sight of the cars and pass your water. Don't you even think about those woods over there, though. You'd be caught. You know it, and the judge would add maybe 5 years to the time you'll spend at Huntsville."

"Yes sir." They stumbled down the bank of the highway till it was level. Billy Joe pissed first, pulling Daryl's hand over to unbutton his levis. Daryl thought about the strangeness of this situation as his hand, cuffed to Billy Joe's, shaded Billy Joe's pecker from the sun.

Billy Joe whispered, without looking at Daryl, "Let's make a run for it. We can leg it down the ditch, then jump the fence down yonder at that gully."

"I don't think we got a chance, Billy. I saw old Wiggins unlimber his gun in his holster. That old coot would like nothing better than to shoot our legs out from under us while we were trying to escape." It was Daryl's turn to piss, now. He had not felt the urge until he had heard Cresson's stream splattering on the sand; then, just as when he was in the woods hunting with his father and his brothers, when one person took a leak, all the others were wont to do so in a shared communal instinct. "He'd only have to hit one of us and the other would go down. Besides, I don't like the idea of being shot at by Stubby Wiggins."

"Yeah, maybe you're right. Even if we made it into the woods, they would get the bloodhounds after us pretty quick."

Daryl shook his weirer with his free hand, shoved it back into his pants, and buttoned them. They turned and walked awkwardly back up the bank where Blake turned the cuffs around, cuffing left to right. As Daryl slid into the car seat, his heart settled into a deep disconsolate mood. There would be no more stops, and his last taste of freedom, a piss in the countryside, had already drained away on the sandy floor of the barditch.

## Chapter IX THE WALLS

*"His vision is so worn from passing bars*
*that bars and only bars are whirled*
*before him. It seems there are a thousand bars*
*before him, and beyond the thousand bars, no world."*

Then they were out of the car. Sam clumsily checked the handcuffs. The immense gray walls thrust up 70 feet from the ground like a feudal dungeon. Later, he was to find that was the name prisoners gave it, simply The Walls. Everyone walked awkwardly towards the little guards shack before the main gates; in the towers, on the corners of the walls stood grim faced men with machine guns. Daryl had never seen machine guns before; no comic books or movies had prepared him for the deadly nausea in the pit of his stomach at the sight of the real machine guns.

As Blake presented his credentials and the court papers to the guards, Daryl's eyes were caught, then riveted to a bronze plaque placed in the grey stone wall. No one seemed to see the plaque but him. Sam had to jerk him roughly by the arm to tear him away from it.

Engraved in the bronze were these words:

ENTER HERE ALL YOU WHO HAVE LEFT
THE LAND OF THE LIVING. KNOW
NOW, YOUR NAME IS LOST.

Way into the night as he lay on the rough bunk, those words remained in his mind as though he saw them in a dream. When at last he slept, he slept fitfully, aware of the least turning of other bodies in the same room. Another dream came to him in the night, in this dream he and many other men were working in long fields, whose rows stretched farther than the eye could see. Above and behind him were men with whips and clubs who kept driving him down the row. His eyes were so blinded by his tears and the fury of his dream, he could not even see what his hands were doing, whether picking or hoeing, he did not know.

That dream was interrupted by a man's scream fading away as though the body behind the voice was falling through space. Dan slowly opened his eyes. The scream was real; he had heard it alright. Many nights sleeping in the woods and being awoken by animals stirring in the brush had honed his ears; he knew when he heard something outside himself. But around him lay only sleeping men, dead to the world. He tried to go back to sleep, but the scream lingered at the threshold of his consciousness. He had a different sense of time, which may be described as being outside of time. Time passed interminably slow, if at all. There was nothing left to anticipate. Whatever was to come would be as bad as they said it was. He was aware that in prison, what happened in the world of time would probably be totally without meaning. What happened inside his head was everything; he had to keep his sanity, even if it meant playing a fool or moron.

Then he slept again, as though the body forced the mind into some instinctual rest where it could recuperate and he dreamt again. This time he was hanging from a cliff with one hand which was being bitten through at the wrist by a jackal. With his other hand he was trying to choke the jackal off his hand. The dream lasted a long time; finally he had choked the jackal's neck through until it consisted of a single cord of sinew. But the head of the jackal maintained its death grip on his wrist. At last he managed to snap the last thread of the jackal's life and he fell from the cliff into a deep abyss where he could sleep and would not dream.

## Chapter X NULL . . . VETO, VOID

*"I have seen the wicked in great power and spreading himself like a green bay tree."*

Two weeks in The Walls was enough for Daryl. They had separated him and Billy Joe, putting them in different wings of the prison. All around him was the fear and smell of death. The scream he heard the first night there was real. An inmate had crawled through an air-vent to the roof, and then slipped or fell three stories to the ground breaking his back and both legs. He lay there all night before they found him.

Another man had killed himself by swallowing razorblades; he bled to death before a doctor ever saw him. Daryl had his toothbrush stolen off his bunk when he turned his back for a second, which didn't ease his paranoia any. Fear was written on every man's face. On the faces of most guards a deep vertical gash indented their brow between their eyes.

Daryl was determined to get sent to the prison farms. Knowing nothing about them he figured he would at least be out in the open, and anything would be better than this living hell at Huntsville. This filled his mind as he was led into the Warden's office for the routine five minute interview given each new prisoner.

"J. D. NULL, WARDEN" read the brass nameplate on the desk. Daryl studied the face intently, that of a man who had filled a role so long that his entire character could be read in the mask. The scrubbed pink ears, the short thin hair and the part in the hair rifle-barrel straight, the tight lips and puffed cheeks of a man who ate much and smiled little. Most noticeable, though, was the vertical crease chiseled deeply between his eyes just like the guards. Truly if there was a mark of Cain, this was it: The hatchet mark between Null's eyes.

Null looked up from the file in front of him. "Barnes you don't have too many marks against you, not yet. Certainly not as many as most of those we keep in lockup. But let me tell you now. You can't afford to do one thing wrong while you're in this prison. We can add to your sentence and add to it, and add . . ." his voice trailed off. The last "add" sounded totally abstract as if it registered only in the deepest recess of his mind. (Later, Daryl would muse that he certainly looked like an "adder.") Daryl knew that he himself meant nothing to Null, that he was no more than the ink-blotter on the desk. "You have something to say boy? Well, speak up."

"Warden Null, I would like to know if I could go—if you would send me to one of the work farms. I've farmed all my life and that's what I know best."

"Hmmmh! Well, I can send you to Sugarland all right. Though the farming there is not like farming you've ever seen. But they can make good use out of you. And, it may do you some good. Of course a lot of men like to get down on the farm because they think it's a good place to escape. You don't have escape on your mind, do you? Good! I didn't think you would. Sure, we can send you down. You will leave next Monday." And the tight mouth clamped shut like a trap. With a wave of his hand he motioned the guard to take Daryl away.

As the bars slid shut behind him, there was only one word rolling over and over on his tongue: Sugarland—Sugarland—Sugar—land—Sugar—.

# Chapter XI SUGARLAND

*"War fathers and rules all things."*

The prison bus skirted the suburbs of Houston, perhaps because to give convicts even a glimpse of city life would be more pleasure than the authorities wished to afford. Finally, the bus rambled through the small town of Sugarland, past the sooty brick buildings emblazoned with the single giant word, IMPERIAL. A likely place to found an empire, this flat coastal plane dotted with thickets of scrub oak. Daryl would soon learn every nuance of that word, *imperial.*

After a couple of miles the bus turned back north abruptly over some railroad tracks down a short road to the prison. The drive from the gates of the prison down to the confinement area proper echoed the word, empire, in Daryl's mind. Here were the guard houses, made of fancy brick comparable to the very best homes in his hometown; here the carefully planted and trimmed live oak trees, row on row, stood like sentinels [Daryl had never believed he could be made to hate a live oak, but then he had never seen any like these that stood so neat and indecent in the way their limbs were artificially clipped and severed to conform to a notion in the mind of some man]. And the grass clipped out in such neat round circles from the trees was St. Augustine grass, indeed an imperial appearance. Daryl saw not one blade unshorn, straggly, or out of place; shortly later he would learn that the task of this mindless manicuring would be one of the most highly prized jobs at the prison; men, certain of losing their minds, will out of instinct, still seeking to preserve the body, search out a path of increased animal ease. Soon, too, Daryl would learn that the unflagging goal of the "bosses" at Sugarland was to break you, mind and body, to geld you, to cut off the roots.

The bus did not go in the main entrance but slid around to the side under the watchful eyes of men in the tower who cradled machine guns in their arms. An electronic switch opened the high barbed fence and the bus rolled to a stop in the concrete yard. The gate slammed shut behind. "Okay, everybody out single file when I give the command! No stragglers, no talking. Keep your mouths shut and do as you're told. Anybody steps out of line will be kissing cement in the *"hole"* in no time. Okay, follow me out after I am out of the bus and on the ground." The lock on the cage in the bus clicked open, and Daryl with 24 other chained men, stepped out with his head shorn into the teeth of a January wind, into another, larger cage.

Two guards approached wearing pistols, one circling in back of the string of men. The other moved down the line unsnapping the cuffs that bound each prisoner to the long chain. Then, backing up ten or twelve feet, "Now it won't take you long to learn the ropes here. Some places you can grabass around and get by with it. Not at Sugarland. The guards in those towers are crack shots with 30-06 Remingtons. They won't stop to ask you if you're just scratching your ass; one false move on your part and they will nail you. And if they just happen to have in their hands at the time one of the Thompsons or the Reisings, then they're likely to cut in half most of the meat in the yard. Most of you are fresh from the transient sector at Huntsville; I see where half of you are on your first term. You won't be green long. What you left was more like a hotel than prison. There you had privileges. Here you have nothing, but what we give you. Here, we give you nothing but your life, and you will keep that only so long as you maintain the perspective that it is we who give it to you. We do not plan to rehabilitate you. All that shit is for the outside. We only plan to keep you till you've served your term, and while we keep you, we work you. Any slackness, any sluggardness, and you hit the *hole*. Once out of the hole, you will work. We don't pass out a list of prison rules here because there's only one rule, and that is *Jump*.

"When you have to piss, you say 'Pour it out here, Boss,' and you don't pour it out until and unless he tells you to.

"Whenever one of the bosses says 'move,' you jump. When he says 'run,' you double-time. When he says 'shit,' you shit."

"Now, take two paces forward and peel off your clothes, shoes, socks, everything, and put it on the ground in front of you. Move!"

Not cold, as far as absolute cold. Just cold, bitter human cold, to stand naked in that cold north wind on the sullen, icy concrete. "Now, about face and two paces, move! Some of you, as we've learned from long years of experience, try to smuggle a little contraband everywhere you go. That's why this skin search. Get used to it. Every working day is a skin search. Each time you leave these walls you will try to sneak something back in even if it's no more than snakeroot or pipeweed. Okay, driver, check those clothes. Now when I walk behind you and say 'spread,' I want you to bend over and spread your cheeks. I'm not looking for dingleberries, just keester plants. Anybody farts in my face, I'm likely to shove a bit of blue steel up that bunghole. Okay. Spread! Spread! Spread! Spread!————

The driver found nothing in the clothes. The guard, satisfied with his inspection of the assholes, strode around in front of the line of quivering, naked men. "All right. You're a bunch of clean assholes. Now, how many of you eat bananas?" Not a man spoke a sound. *"Goddamnit!* Answer me! How many eat bananas?" Twenty-five hands shot into the air in unison.

"That's better. You'd think I asked if you sucked cocks. Well, most of you do that, too, or will. Only cocksuckers find their way into prison. Now when I give the word, *Peel!,* I want all of you to reach down with both hands and peel back that foreskin just like you peel bananas. Most of you are southern country boys and didn't have a Jew doctor around to whittle on your pecker. Some of you have never taken a bath and you've got 21 years of head cheese accumulated. Others, perhaps one or two of you, thought you could sneak money or a balloon or two of smack into the prison with a rubber band. Well, we'll find out. Peel!"

Fifty hands quickly obeyed the order, so stricken with fear and humiliation, they no longer knew it was humiliation. The guard had repeated this ritual so often, he peeled out the command, Peel!, like some archbishop of Rome telling a lowly peasant to kneel. No dope, no money dripped from the penises, but one gaunt boy, thin-face and haggard, loosed a trickle of yellow steaming piss onto the cold concrete. From the guard's long years of experience he knew this, too, was often part of the ritual. He smiled briefly at the sight of the yellow stream puddling on the concrete. Walking toward the youth, he slid his club—euphemistically called a baton—

made of second-growth hickory from his belt. With a suddenness that surprised even himself, he popped the youth on the tip of his cock with the club, snapping his wrist downward. The sharp cry of the young man at the numbing pain, though muffled, shot through the hearts of everyone standing there. Daryl felt his buttocks twitch with an old memory of sitting on a bull nettle; his pecker tried to shrink up into his body. The youth who was struck would piss only with pain for over a month.

"First lesson on movement by the numbers. Yot not only jump when we say "move." You halt till we say go. You don't even piss till it's time to. Any man who can't hold his water will learn to, or he will end up in the infirmary. Now put on those clothes. Move!"

Daryl did not feel his hands touch the clothes; he only saw himself and the other men dress faster than they had undressed. He was already beginning not to think when the file of men turned to trot through the narrow door into the bowels of the prison where he would spend at least one year or two years and maybe his whole life.

## Chapter XII BONES

*"Reality outran apprehension."*

Likely Sugarland would have ground Daryl into dust had it not been for a man named William Bone. There is no adequate place to begin describing Bone, or "Bones" as he was called; each encounter with the man left an indelible imprint in the mind. Daryl saw him first in the mess hall the evening of his first day there; he was eating the pinto beans, cornbread and cane syrup like a wolf, his eyes not watching the food, but surveying the whole room. He saw every nuance on every face.

Deepset eyes, a bright fierce dark which almost forbade a closer look into them for a bit of color; these were set upon high cheekbones that spoke of his probable Indian blood—that and the almost beardless chin; but his nose was straight, an English nose which sculptured the air like chiseled marble; the mouth hard but not cruel, and all these features beneath a shock of coal-black hair, which being barbered prison-fashion [shaved in back at ear level] gave him more the look of a bird, some wild hawk, than a man.

They said he'd been sent up for murder, had killed a man, an off-duty sheriff, in a fight over a woman down in Alpine. It was also said that he was sent up because the D.A. in Alpine hated him and framed him, when he had killed in self-defense, which is true of many, if not most, men in prison, and some women. They are there, not for the wrong they have done, but because they possess some primal sense of freedom, which the so-called settled or civilized man finds intolerable and will thus turn and turn the law, that barbarous absolute, until the one free of the law is caught in its snares.

So Bones was one of these. Even there in prison, it was an odd question to ask who was more free: Bones or the prison guards. True, Bones was enslaved, yet every ounce of his being, each quick step he took, pronounced a sense of freedom and ability to act, which was foreign to the guards with their thin pursed lips and their foreheads fixed in deep lines of fear.

Bones took it on himself to break in a new man to the Sugarland routine. He did this by working beside the new man whether in the fields, the cannery, or at drill, with short choppy sentences almost under his breath. They were short declarations which told you the exact nature of the job, how far you could push a guard, a *bull,* before he would turn on you, and how to twist the bull by the tail when you were desperate. He never bothered to ask what one thought of his advice. He gave it; the other took it. He assumed the newcomer already knew he was in the brotherhood of the damned, and that mere survival demanded razor wits and a tempered will. One of the first things he mentioned was who the "yardbirds" were, the "stoolies" who were getting some "juice" from the guards in return for information on their fellow convicts. He would say curtly, "You talk too much at chow; button your lip," or "Don't talk to Stroud; he'll burn you for a pack of cigarettes or a blow job."

There was no doubt in Daryl's mind that Bones could have escaped any time he wanted to. He was serving a twenty-to-life, and had done four years already. Anytime it was mentioned, someone invariably whispered that if he ever caught the first train out, he would take a lot of bodies with him. It's true that Bones was a sort of glue that kept a lot of hard-timers from breaking under the strain of the forced work and the numbing fear of the beatings by the guards.

Daryl never did see Bones smile except when he talked to Connors. But then, Connors could make a stone statue crack a grin. Connors was a black man, tall, broad-shouldered, with powerful arms and hands. The blacks were separated then in the quarters to keep down fights, but they were thrown together with whites and Mexicans to pick cotton or okra, or work in the cannery. Also they were allowed to participate in the prison rodeo in the summertime, that made for beautiful public relations when the thousands of civilians who came to the prison rodeo saw the black and white convicts mingling together, no doubt leading some fool tourists to say: "well, ain't that something. Look how good those colored boys act when they are in prison and participating in something like this rodeo."

Connors was from Pampa out on the plains and was a crack rodeo man; he could ride and dog the bulls, and ride the bareback broncs, but his specialty was calf-roping. Connors was much like Bones, struck from the same mold but perhaps the obverse side of the coin. He had few enemies among the prisoners because his ever-ready smile, that quick ivory gleam in the wide ebony face, lifted a lot of burdens even from the hearts of some of the dyed-in-the-wool bastards.

That spring when they first shipped Daryl down to Sugarland from The Walls, there wasn't much to do for two months but cut weeds. They farmed them out in road gangs of about twenty men each to cut with a yo-yo sling the chest high Johnson grass which choked the country roads around Sugarland after the spring rains. With each road gang went a straw-boss armed with a pistol and a whip and two outriders on horseback with Winchester rifles. The outriders never got close enough for anyone to see their faces; their orders were simply to shoot and kill any convict who tried to escape.

One of the days, three roadgangs were thrown together to clear some brush down close to the tracks, which, it was rumored, would be turned into another cotton field. Since the men were given axes to chop the trees and bushes, the guard was increased. Everywhere Daryl looked, he saw a rifle barrel flash in the cold sunlight!

Even though it was a cold March day, the thermometer struggling to hit 55 degrees, Daryl and most others had worked up a heavy sweat by mid-morning. Once sweating like a horse, Daryl was afraid to slow down for fear of catching a chill and coming down with pneumonia. Only Bones showed no sign of exertion or the arduousness of the work. His lean wiry arms swung the axe like a toothpick, rhythmically slashing away at the brush, laying the edge of the blade exactly right at the foot of the saplings of sumac and scrub oak.

Connors, for some reason had moved slightly out of his road gang over to where he could talk to Bones as he swung his axe. Daryl, just off to the left, overheard most of what they said.

"Hey you, Billy Bones!"

"Hey what, Con-Roy."

"When you gettin' out-a-here?"

"Quittin' time. Yourself?"

"Naw, I mean when you gonna—catch the train?"

"Why Con-Roy, I like it here."

"Sure, and pigs like shit, too. No, Bones, when you gonna jump loose?"

But Connors was the one who jumped! Bone's axe looked like it would cleave Connors' foot, but buried itself in the brush. As Connors leaped up in the air, a guard nearby jacked a cartridge into the chamber of his 30-30 Marlin. Everybody dropped their axes and froze except Bones who dived into the brush. In a few seconds he emerged grinning, holding a five foot Eastern Diamondback rattler, as thick as his arm, its head neatly chopped off by the axe-stroke Connors had thought was aimed for his foot.

The guard relaxed at the sight of the rattler, and spoke. "Bring 'im here, Bones. I'll clip that rattle and give it to my boy."

"Yes sir, boss. He's a big 'un, ain't he?"

"Pretty damn big, Bones. He was about to get Connors by the leg, wasn't he."

"Yes sir, boss. Though if it'd bit him, bin the snake'd died."

"Haw! Haw! Yep. I reckon rattlers wouldn't like that black meat no more than they like hog meat. Goddamn! Twelve rattlers and a button. That was an old Granddad you laid the axe to, Bones."

"I reckon so, boss."

"Okay, you yardapes. Enough gawking. Pick your pieces and lay at that wood. I want to hear those bushes sing and whistle as they fall."

Bones slid back into the ragged rank alongside Connors. Connors was busting with excitement and could barely keep his big gleaming grin suppressed.

"Lord! Lord! Thought you'd done chopped my leg off."

"I would have, too, if that snake had got a hold of it. And you'd have thanked me for it."

"He, he, heee! Now you just got to tell me Bones. When you gonna jump on that train."

"Aw—maybe when the river's good and warm."

"Ha! Ha! I bet you will. I suspect I will, too."

"What's your ticket Con-Roy?"

"Me? Why I got me a rodeo ticket. Shore nuff. I'm gonna calf rope my freedom."

"And make old Null holler 'calfrope?' "

"Yep, I'll deal that son of a bitch the eight of spades."

Along about two in the afternoon, Daryl took a glance over his shoulder to see how far they'd come. If anybody had told him beforehand that sixty men could have flattened all that brush he would have thought them loco. Then, off to the right another commotion erupted. A thin dark little Cajun came jumping out with a two-foot rattler in his hand, yelling "He bit me boss! He bit me!"

"Drop it on the ground, Santerre. Lay that snake down."

"Yes sir, boss."

The guard jacked one in, aimed, and drilled the snake through the head, the echo of the shot rocking down the river bottom. "Now, come here, Santerre, you little devil."

"He bit me boss. It wasn't my fault."

"The hell it wasn't." The guard sheathed his rifle, drew out his pocket knife and made two quick slashes across the snakebite on Santerre's arm. "Now you get your carcass back to sickbay, you hear. Boots, take this one back to the doc at a quick jog." And Santerre, his arm dripping blood, loped away, hurried along by the big Morgan mare on his heels.

Daryl turned to Bones. "Won't that kill him, all that running?"

"Naw. It was just a baby rattler. He let it bite him on purpose. Gets 2 weeks in a sickbay everytime he's bit. Santo has built up immunity by now; he's been bit over twenty-five times. Last summer he didn't even report two times he was bit cause he feared they thought he was getting too much time off. He was right."

## Chapter XIII SUNDAY SERVICES

*"Yes, they whipped him up the hill for me."*

Come Sunday, and they crowded in the prison chapel for services. Two hours till visitors could come, bringing their chocolate cakes, their smiles, their tears, their bare faces in unrelieved recognition of home.

Daryl didn't expect visitors for months. His folks were short on money. But they would be down here, and if they couldn't come they would write. The first letter he got from them at Sugarland brought hot scalding tears to his eyes; the simplest phrase, "I patched your red jacket" tore loose the dam in his heart and it all welled up in his throat and eyes. He wasn't able to write much in reply: a few lines like, "I'm O.K. We have to work hard here. There're some older convicts, who are not bad men, to show me the ropes. They feed us well. Don't worry no more than you can help it. Love, your son, Daryl."

The churchhouse in the jailhouse shocked Daryl with its simplicity and lack of ornamentation. The bare pews bolted to the floor, the unvarnished pulpit on a narrow elevated platform, and the two windows looking out crisscrossed with bars let him know he was still in jail. The row upon row of prisoners with their close-cropped hair, freshly shaven well above the ears, sitting still and straight on the stiff pews made him think of a vegetable garden, the sunburnt backs of the necks red like beets.

The songbooks were passed around. Many had pages torn or cut out. When the singing started, Daryl felt chills run up his spine. Some element of doom, some sense of hopelessness, buried deep by 72 hours of back-breaking work in the shadow of a gun had sunk to the bottom of reckoning in the men's minds and now came slowly, tortuously to the surface like some Cartesian diver. The songs were sung slow and emphatic; each syllable rang like iron on an anvil.

Oh land of rest,<br>
For thee I sigh—<br>
When will the moment come—<br>
We'll wor-rk—<br>
    till Je-sus comes,<br>
We'll wor-rk—<br>
    til Je-sus comes.<br>
We'll wor-rk<br>
    til Jee-sus comes<br>
Then we'll<br>
    be gathered home—.

Their voices quavering on words like work until Daryl did not hear, did not feel the word at all, but only felt the numbing pain of the week's toil gathered and hurled towards heaven. The word, "home," hit and held in some ground bass, reverberated long after the song was done. Daryl was to learn that the prisoners only sang a few dozen of the songs in the book, though it held a few hundred; These were those that had the most power, almost hypnotic power, those that could bring release.

A-ma-a-a-zing Grace,
How sweet—the sound—
That saved—a-a wretch
LIKE ME!
I once wa-as lost,
But now am found,
Was chained but now
AM FREE!

After working their way through a half dozen songs, the air was different. There was more breath in the air. On cue, a short, fat, banty-legged preacher walked up behind the pulpit.

"Amen! Amen, brethren. Now is there any man here who is not a sinner. No, not one of us is without sin, for we have all sinned and fallen short of the glory of God. For so we are told in God's Holy Word. And none of us shall find pardon until we turn to God's Holy Word and there seek out the glory and grace of our Lord Jesus Christ.

Jesus said, "I am not come into the world to bring peace, but a sword." No there is no peace in this world, brethren. There is only a sword. Peace, the peace that passeth understanding, is ours only when we quit the walks of this life."

Daryl, his eyes wide open, had sealed his ears; his memory drifted to scenes on the river as a boy with his father, a peace the preacher knew nothing about. The day of rest passed quickly as in a dream.

## Chapter XIV OKRA

Daryl's folks didn't get to come visit for a few months, having no money to make the trip. But they wrote steady, humble letters that sustained him. The work was backbreaking; some days his body was so numb he no longer recognized it. On top of the heavy workload stood the fury that drove everyone, the fear of death that grew from the murderous spite of the guards.

Bones had shown him a simple ritual that kept him from breaking under the threats and taunts of the guards. The danger lay in the normal human wrath that longs to strike back; if anyone jumped a guard—and sometimes they did—he would be beaten unmercifully first, then tossed into solitary, the hole where they starved the guts out of you. The ritual was this; when Daryl felt ready to crack under the strain, he would yell out, "Lightin' up here, boss," then hunker down and steady his hands enough to roll a Bull Durham cigarette, and say to himself, "You won't be here forever; this little cigarette's gonna help you do your time." Many was the time, though, when they were on the line chopping cotton, that such was not allowed, and his only escape was to become part of the hoe that kept grabbing at the earth.

At times the awareness flashed through Daryl's mind that the main crop at Sugarland was not corn, not cotton, not cane, tomatoes, okra nor hay. No, the main crop was men. Here men were ground down to the germ of the corn and the germ itself was buried in black alluvial dirt. There was no stronger way to break a man's spirit than to work him into the dirt until he felt he was no better than the dirt he walked upon.

Okra season came, and everyone picked okra. Not merely for the messhall was the picking done. Nine out of every ten pounds was canned at the cannery and sold to a commercial distributor who merely pasted his own labels on the prison okra. If the company had to print on their label: "This okra was picked by men in prison who were paid a dime a day for their labor," who would buy that okra off the shelf?

To pick the okra they were issued one pair of heavy duty gloves. When the fingers of the gloves wore out, the gloves were turned inside out and the insides of the backs of the fingers of the gloves were used. When that side wore out and all that was left of the fingers of the gloves was the seam running up the side, and the fingers were bleeding raw from the okra, the pods were gathered in the palm of the hand. The part of the glove that covered the palm was also soon eaten away by the omnivorous okra. No new gloves were issued. Once they had picked through the fields of okra, the plants had pushed out fresh pods, and they started over at the first row. Even the tough salty okra plants bent before the driven fury of the prisoners; after the third picking the pods were so spotty, they plowed the stalks under. The gloves, many of which barely covered the heel of the hand, were turned back in. The hands of the pickers healed; they had to heal before the cotton season came.

## Chapter XV A VIEW FROM THE TABERNACLE

One hundred and fifty miles from Sugarland, the town of Austin straddles the Colorado River. Two buildings tower over the landscape: the state capitol hewn out of red granite found up close to Marble Falls and the library tower on the campus of the University of Texas. To get the money to buy the rock for the steep domed capitol, the politicians had sold off ten Texas counties to English bankers, which formed the basis for the old XIT spread; XIT stands for Ten in Texas. The University tower as well as most other buildings were built with oil found on public lands trusted to the college.

The same spring that Daryl Barnes and Billy Joe Cresson were shipped to Central I and Central II, a certain Professor Tompson was lecturing on Texas history to a small class of undergraudates. Tompson was a curious sort of man; no doubt, it was difficult to be an intellectual in Texas then as much as at any other time. He styled his hair with the same rifle-barrel part high on the right side as he had seen one time in a photo of William James. Though he'd only been to St. Louis once and New Orleans twice, he assidulusly studied catalogs and magazines to ascertain the latest ivy league styles and dressed accordingly. His gestures, too, were studied, slow and deliberate; one would not have guessed he was born in Copperas Cove, Texas.

Today, he sensed that few of his students were paying attention. The sun was out after a week of rain, and the sharp smells of early spring were sapping any intellectual resolve the students might have had.

"Well, now let us look at some of the reasons 'Pa' Ferguson fell from grace as governor of Texas, and why his wife was elected in his place. Bear in mind the four dominant political forces and the two that were building. First, you had the oil money, new and rapacious. Spindletop blew all hell out of that utopian dream of agrarian paradise that Moses and Stephen Austin had brought down from Virginia where they had shared it with Madison, Jefferson and Monroe.

"So you had these $1,000 a month lobbyists strutting through that capitol building over there touting the *worthy* cause of Mr. Rockefeller or some other potentate. And their lobbying was furious. If you remember, when Ida Tarbell—and I ask you, is Tarbell not the finest and fittest poetic name for the first and best muckraker the oil industry has ever seen—anyway when she published her book outlining in livid detail the methods Mr. Rockefeller and his hirelings used to eat up competition, the furor which ensued and the anti-trust action actually led to Standard Oil being banned from Texas for a few short years. Of course, they were soon back in the state—some say, after they had bought off the state's Attorney General who had first driven them from Texas. They came back with a new name and new faces, but it was the same old Rockefeller money; their new name was Humble Oil.

Now, what finer name could they have chosen to gull the hardshell Baptists, Methodists and Campbellites than "Humble." None, I tell you. It was a masterpiece of Onomatopoeia. At any rate, they were out for a few years and the independents had grown considerably in finance capital and sagacity; when Standard in the guise of Humble crept back into the fold they found a pack of wolves where there had been sheep. So the oil lobbyists were fast and furious in buying up the state legislators and shrinking them to fit in their pockets. One chronicler of the age suggested that Texas lawmakers of the time "were the cleanest, honest, most decent men in the country—until they got to Austin." There, the transformation was remarkable.

Incidentally, the feud between the Texas oilmen and the easterners continues to this day; that's why Texas, as country-bumpkin and out of the way as it is, exerts a power over national politics in the human forms of Mister Sam Rayburn in the house and Lyndon Johnson in the Senate that is surpassed only—and that just by a hair—by the New York crowd gathered around the Rockefellers. Mr. Dulles, for instance, and his firm are the main corporate lawyers for the Rockefellers. The time has not arrived when Texas can name the President. As an example, see how Roosevelt dropped John Nance Garner from the ticket on the third term. But it will come someday soon, and then Texas is likely to have as long a string of Presidents as did once the old Dominion of Virginia.

But I digress. In back of the oilmen stood an older, cannier bunch, the railroads. By controlling the state Railroad Commission, as well as most legislators, they controlled every major decision made regarding public lands. By and large their interests coincided with the oil interests but when they did not, the railroads at that point still held the upper hand. The boom of World War I with its movement of troops and supplies had added enormously to the wealth of the railroads.

Alongside of these were the old cattlemen; though they did not know it, they already stood in the shadow of the waning moon. The railroads had leveled doom on their way of life as surely as it spelled the end of the buffalo and the Plains Indians. With railroads running all through Texas, a rancher didn't need a tenth the number of cowhands it took to trail a herd to Kansas. The railroads also moved the cattle industry north and east and left Texas with only a large but steadily diminishing slice of pie. Yet there was a toughness to these cattlemen; they were as tough as whet leather, as ornery as a longhorn bull. The best and shrewdest of them went into politics, as they saw that as the best way of preserving their way of life. The Klebergs and Cactus Jack Garner are the prime examples.

But the real political strength lay in the small farmers who had fanned up the Texas rivers after the War Between the States, buying or renting their own quarter sections of bottom land and working it with only a team of mules, a plowhorse and a passel of kids. Most of these were English or Scoth-Irish, fundamentalist Protestant, almost as heavy for Prohibition as the old cattle empires were against it. Their strength has dwindled now, but around the turn of the century they were the whirlwind to be reckoned with. After the panic of 1873, the control of the railroads, and the stock market, and the buying and selling of commodities passed into fewer and fewer hands. This control of the farm produce, how it got to market and the price it was sold for, led to the populist revolts in the South and the West. The last populist governor that Texas had, who could be said to accurately convey this fierce democratic spirit was Jim Hogg. When Governor Altgeld of Illinois was threatening to intervene on the side of the railroad strikers, Hogg offered to put at Altgeld's disposal a thousand Texas Rangers, and he was very nearly taken up on the offer. Probably the threat of federal intervention was what took the steam out of Altgeld's sails. But, as I was saying, Hogg was the last and the finest of the Populist governors. His kind will not come again.

Now by Ferguson's time in office there are stirrings of that same fierce populism, around certain farm problems, banking practices, and the old demon of prohibition. *"Are you fer it or agin it."* Most of these bible belt farmers were so dead set against the "drink" and such firebrands in their sermons upon it, historians called them "Anglo-Evangelicals." Contrast them with the Germans, Czechs, and Russian immigrants that settled here. Whereas their interests were almost the same as the Anglo farmers, their views on alcoholic beverages were opposite. The longevity of their predisposition towards stimulating drink which they brought from Europe has no finer example than Scholz's beergarden, certainly an institution of Austin, yea even of the whole state of Texas.

So we see Ferguson now, elected by an amalgam of support: railroad money behind him, populist rhetoric in front of him. Once into office, he was perhaps no more or less corrupt than every other governor we have had since 1906. But he had some idiosyncracies. He believed a good portion of his populist rhetoric. For one thing he moved against the banks. But what really angered and infuriated the upper crust and equally tickled and pleased the little man was Ferguson's attitude towards prisoners on the state prison farms. The first two decades of the century had seen Texas prison population swell enormously. The oil boom had brought a lot of fortune-seekers, commonly called riff-raff, into the state. Old Europe was bursting at the seams and many of its poorer citizens and refugees sought a better life in the U.S., many working their way to Texas. Also, many native sons had served a hitch under old Black Jack Pershing in France; a taste of French wine and French women had spoilt them, you might say, for the homespun pleasures of the Texas frontier, and when they returned from the war they were a hard lot to deal with. Especially with the onset of Prohibition.

So, the prison ranks grew, and the state penitentiary, efficient as it was, turned the convicted felons to useful work, picking cotton and cutting sugar cane on prison farms still in use over near Sugarland on the Brazos River. Now that was a rough prison farm in those days, class. Those canebrakes held Diamondback rattlers thick as a man's arm. Between the snakes and the fights, many prisoners and not a few guards left Sugarland in pine coffins. Nowadays, they no longer cut the cane by hand, but they still pick the cotton by hand, even though there's machines to do that, too.

So Ferguson is plagued with letters from relatives of those convicts about conditions down there on the Brazos. He learns that the letters are by and large factual accounts of what took place down there, so he started to pardon a lot of the convicts. The controversy began to rage; as Ferguson saw his popularity climb as he released more prisoners, the more frequently he would use any excuse such as a holiday like Thanksgiving, Christmas or Easter to issue a raft of pardons. Shortly, there were barely enough convicts to keep the main prison at Huntsville running, and few to maintain the profitable plantation down on the Brazos. So people began to organize against Ferguson, particularly people with money who didn't cotton to the idea of so many thieves running around loose after serving only a few months of their terms.

So, you know the text. Ferguson was impeached by the legislature on charges of bribery. Yet he was so popular that his wife, Miriam or 'MA' Ferguson, was elected to serve out his term in the special election and then reelected in her own right. It was mainly these dirt farmers who elected her. Undoubtedly Ferguson's leniency with convicted felons had been a popular idea with the little man.

The governor who beat MA Ferguson out was Pat Neff. Neff vowed that he would pardon absolutely no one all the time he was in office. Well, a very famous blues and country singer by the name of Huddie Ledbetter had got into a knife fight down in Houston after singing in a bar, killed the other fellow, and received a life sentence. "Leadbelly," as he is often known, had already gained a considerable reputation as the best Texas-styles blues guitar man around, and there were a lot of them around. The able folklorist and musician, John Lomax, came to find out that "Lead" was in prison, and that he had already been sent to Sugarland to pick cotton. By the way, there's truth to the story that Leadbelly on a few occasions picked a thousand pounds of cotton a day, which is about *two* bales. Well, Lomax gains an audience with the governor, Neff, and persuades him, very reluctantly, to at least hear Leadbelly play his twelve-string guitar, before he said a final *no* on a pardon. The rest is history. Leadbelly was hauled up to Austin in chains, and when he was through playing, Neff pardoned him on the spot.

I brought along this poem, which tells the story with perhaps more feeling. Here, pass this out . . .

HUDDIE LEDBETTER

Whip it on down,<br>
Huddie!<br>
Ten thick fingers<br>
Whanging a twelve-stringer.

Where we had two chords
in our voice-box,
You had twelve;
Where we had one heart
You had ten
Throbbing and bursting
Inside your chest,
Where Pity and Passion
played with a guitar pick.

Whang it on down, Huddie!
Lord, the air's so
thick with your music,
The good ache of it
forgets me all my blues.

Sing to me of Sugarland
and cotton pickin'
On the Brazos.
A thousand pounds a day!
Lord, sing that again!
A thousand pounds a day!

*"You got to jump around*
*a bit to pick that much."*

What the dude in Houston
didn't know, Huddie,
Was this: your belly's made
Of iron, not lead,
And when he had his knife
In your belly,
And you had your knife
In his belly,
your belly
Was made of iron, and

His was not, no,
His belly was not made of
Iron.
The saying ain't so, that
what you don't know
won't hurt you. It's good to know
That Leadbelly
Was made of iron.

What songs did you sing
For the old governor,
Pat Neff,
That day to make him
Set you free.
Huddie, what songs did you sing?
Did you sing, "I got stripes,"
Or "Yaller Gal," or
"Like a turkey through the corn
With his Long johns on."
No matter,
you set
Yourself free,
Bunching your hands
And whanging
On your guitar,
Your big flat-bottomed
12-string Blues guitar.

Let me chip this in stone
for you, Huddie.
You still be
the top bottle
On the blue-bottle tree.

*"Yes, they whipped him*
*Up the hill for me!"*

Neff was to pardon only two more people in his two terms in office. Though W. Lee (Pappy) O'Daniel was to revive shades of the Fergusons' populism with his string band playing "O Beautiful Texas" and passing out hot biscuits at all his political rallies, he hewed to a conservative line on prisons, what's now called a "law and order" line. Ever since Neff, you could say the prison industry has become another growth industry in the booming state of Texas."

"Yes, question?"

"Professor, did you say 'blooming' state of Texas?"

"Ha! Ha! Quite a pun. I'm sure they would enjoy that down at Sugarland what with all the cotton blooms amid what they call the blooming Johnson grass. Well, that will be all for today. I hope some of this has sunk in. Remember, there are still thousands like Leadbelly down there on that plantation, being whipped up that hill. . . ."

## Chapter XVI JOHNSON GRASS

"Blooming Johnson grass. I'll be damned if I ever hoe another weed again if I get out of here. Let the damn weeds take over the planet." Daryl was muttering to himself as he strove to maintain the 'line.' The line of twenty cotton choppers moved through the rows in unison, as a machine made of human parts. The oil for the machine was the fear of death that flowed unseen from the barrels of the rifles cradled in the arms of the two men on horseback. The only distinctive human configuration to the flow of the machine came when a convict kicked his head sideways to sling the swirl of streaming sweat out of his eyes. The kicking motion implied a camshaft working in the head that kept them from ever being totally machine, that indicated the primal concern of animal flesh for the sake of the flesh. Otherwise, the hoes swung in unison.

Daryl fancied sometimes it was the Johnson grass biting the hoe rather than the hoe biting it. Each stalk had two to four white snake-like roots as long as the forearm or longer. It wouldn't do to just chop off the thigh deep weeds at the ground; the herd boss, failing to see the white roots gleaming in the sun, would lay his quirt onto the negligent back with a fury. The Johnson grass roots pulled so hard on the hoe Daryl felt his arms constantly being rooted to the ground, the violently uprooted, then just as violently rooted again. The cords in his back, neck and arms stretched, tightened, and relaxed; he would not know what *sore* was until he awoke in the middle of the night to the cry of his body letting go of the ache of the day's pain.

He long ago realized that the main crop at Sugarland, at Ferguson's farm and all the other farms was not cotton, not okra, not tomatoes, and not sugar cane. The main crop was men. Men, beaten, broken and driven into the dirt. As they were broken into the realm of the worker ants and the lizards that eat the ants, not all the seed was plowed into the dirt: the germ escaped into the air and lingered as a pale cast of beauty and life that outshone the neatly clipped St. Augustine grass and the obsessively trimmed oak trees that led up to the prison. This distilled essence, the presence of men in bondage, never deserts a place where it happened. The whole South is permeated with the smell of its prisons like the scent of wisteria.

Time, especially, became difficult for Daryl to reckon. Sure, winter and springtime had passed, and summer come, but he did not see them. He seldom had a clear unobstructed look up at the sky. Once or twice the cry of a wild goose high overhead pierced his ears. Time was measured more in his sleep than in his waking hours. In his dreams in his troubled sleep during the short time allotted to rest his bones the Johnson grass would sometimes win, pulling him face down into the ground.

## Chapter XVII ROLLING A BULL-DURHAM

William Bone provided the glue, the raw meat of courage, that kept many from breaking apart. The fear of death that hung like sex from the barrels of the guard's guns mixed with the brutal punishing work under the boiling Texas sun often broke men's spirits like matchsticks. When they were working the fields, a battered old Studebaker pickup was used to dump the bodies of those who passed out in the blazing heat. When the pickup was full and headed to the barn, they dragged the fallen ones out to lie in the roadbed.

One smooth talker from Dallas, a check artist, couldn't bear to have his hands torn apart by the grinding hoe. On the second day out he threw the longhandle down and walked defiantly towards a boss, muttering "I quit. I ain't no goddamned field nigger." The boss swung his cane at his knees cutting him down.

"Get up and pick up that hoe."

"No!"

Whack!–Whack!–Whack!

"Get up."

"No.–Oh, Damn, god damn almighty. No. Don't please."

"Jake, come over here. Here's one for the Hole. He thinks he's too slick a prick to chop cotton."

Eleven days later and twenty pounds lighter the young Dallas sharpie emerged from the darkened shack, his body weak and thin, his spirit curiously enough strong and determined. When he refused again to go to the fields, they threw him back in the Bucket. After thirty days of refusing most of the stale white bread and water offered once a day, (spam added every 3rd day) they carried him from the shack with the four by four floor to a waiting ambulance. Daryl never saw him again.

Billy Bones, when he could, would spit a few words in newcomers' ears to keep them out of the Hole. He had often talked to Daryl over the standard pinto beans and cornbread supper. "Do your time like a red ant climbing a hill, one clod of dirt at a time. Think no more of the bulls than you would a nest of yellow jackets, but think no less. Don't go sticking your hand in their nose to see if you can do it. They don't need a license to kill on this farm. I've been here almost five years, seen a dozen men die, and not one of the killers even lost his job."

"What did they send you up for, Bones?"

"I killed a man."

Daryl paused, knowing he shouldn't ask the next question, yet sensed that if he asked it, Bones would answer. So, he shifted ground.

"When do you expect you'll get out."

"Never, unless I cut my own row."

"My daddy says that you can kill a man in Texas and get out of the pen in ten years. He says the people they really go after are dopeheads like that stripper Candy Barr. What did she get, 9 years for 3 marijuana cigarettes?"

"Yeah, that's generally true. But the man I killed was a deputy sheriff."

"Oh!"

Later, in the Ballpark, the barren lounge where the

prisoners whiled away their few idle minutes before lockup, Bones showed Daryl how to improve on rolling a smoke.

"First off, the reason for rolling it right is so you don't waste tobacco. Behind that is the reason for smoking Bull-Durham rather than ready-mades. Neither you nor your folks have got enough money to keep you in ready-mades, and the only way you can get that in here is to spend time in the Barrel sucking somebody's cock or getting cornholed. You're paid 10 cents a day and you get that 60 cents every Saturday and usually spend it all on Sunday. If you're tolerant you can get by on one sack of Bull-Durham a week and save the other fifty cents. If you don't save that, you will have nothing to show for all the time you did here. Absolutely nothing. If you want sweets, write and tell your mother or sweetheart to send you cookies every Sunday. These bastards count on 90% of the 6,000 prisoners on this farm to spend all of that 60 cents every Sunday. Figure it up for yourself. That's better than $3,000 a week or $150,000 a year and these jokers clear at least half that. That's just on cigarettes and candy over the counter. The guards can and will sell you cigarettes, tobacco, cocaine, bennies or even a little junk through Toad Anders, the squirrel that keeps the hounds and sleeps outside the gate in that shack. And the prison system as a whole makes an untold fortune off the cotton and the canned okra and tomatoes that goes out of here. You don't want to put a piddling penny more in the pockets of these bastards unless you can help it. That's why you got to learn to roll 'em right. Keep your hands steady. That's it. Lay your finger in there. Now the tobacco. Now lick both edges of the paper. Couldn't have done better myself." And he smiled.

## Chapter XVIII A BULL CALLED MIDNIGHT

*"What are we. What are we not. The Shadow of a Day is Man, no more. But when the brightness comes, and God gives it, there is a shining of light on Man and his Life is sweet."*

Hoeing cotton and picking okra filled up most of June, and into July. In July the prison rodeo at Huntsville began, continuing on every Sunday through the prickling sweat heat of August. Everybody at Sugarland who cared to do so either rode in the rodeo or packed the prison buses to go and watch from the high-fenced pen near the chutes.

Those who savored the contact with horse-flesh, with cowhide, the roar of the thirsty crowd, and the outlet for a venom, a charged fury, that was denied release at the prison farms. In the past, some of the best cowhands in Texas had done time, and the Texas Prison Rodeo had a reputation for being one of the wildest, roughest rodeos around. The stock, especially the Brahmas and the broncs were the raunchiest stock they could find. The inmates pitched into it with a blind recklessness; what the hell, a broken collarbone meant two weeks out of the Line and into the infirmary.

Daryl had decided he would at least ride a bull on the first Sunday out. He didn't have a lot of spare energy on Sundays, no, that wasn't it, but his hands were tough and calloused from the hoeing, and nine seconds, considered in the abstract, seemed no more than a long-drawn breath.

That first Sunday, the Texas summer had begun in earnest. It was 85 degrees when everyone filled the buses at Sugarland, 95 by the time they got to Huntsville, and pushing 105 by the one p.m. starting time for the first horse out of the gate. Luckily it was a dry heat; man and animal alike could sweat freely. The rodeo clowns by the end of the long afternoon would be so drenched that as they made their feints before the bulls, drops of sweat would pop off their heads like flies.

The stock was mean, and the prisoners were coming into it cold—Null had never dreamed of letting anyone practice up—few riders hung on till the buzzer sounded. Among the calf ropers, only Connors stood out. Making up for his slow horse, his rope snaked way out to snare the calf's head, Connors leaping to the ground, throwing and tieing the calf so adroitly the crowd burst into a long low roar of approval; each flashback in their minds convinced them they had just seen some exceptional roping.

Finally Daryl's turn came to straddle the 1200 pound black Brahma bull. Two mates had to grab its ears until it would settle enough for him to get ahold of the rope around its girth. Then the chute flew open and he was dancing in the air on the back of the churning bull. This one was a twister who wore the name of Cyclone. Daryl knew how bad he hurt now, his bones jarring against the swirling bones beneath him, and knew he would hurt worse later, but he drilled all his strength and will into the grip of his right hand curled into the rope. Seconds passed. Daryl had hardly begun to think "this is a good ride" before Cyclone straightened his twisting pitch, kicked his rear legs high and sent Daryl sailing straight over his horns. As he hit the ground, he dimly heard the buzzer over, in back of, and far away from the snorting bull behind him. He rolled to one side, and the clown, the high priest of the Sunday rodeo, with his hand already twisting the tail of the Cyclone, turned the tide. The 1200 pounds of the black beast out of India missed Daryl by a foot.

Back in the prisoners' pen Daryl slid in where Bones had saved him a seat. When he looked up at Bones, the steady black eyes smiled back over the whisper, "it was a good ride."

The final event of the rodeo was the most dramatic. No other rodeo in the Americas has an event to compare with it. As naked confrontation between man and beast, not even the corridos of the Spanish bullfight can compare. No one knows how it came to be a part of the Texas Prison Rodeo; the best guess is that it arose after the legendary black cowboy, Bill Pickett, on a bet, grabbed a wild bull by the horns, swung his legs around the bull's neck and rode it for twenty minutes in a rodeo in Mexico City. The crowd reportedly rioted and stormed through the streets burning stalls and fighting the Federales. Pickett barely escaped the mob with his hide intact; the government of Mexico never invited him back. To this day no one can find an eye witness report as to how Pickett got off that bull.

The crowd today was tense and restless. Except for Connors' roping and a few good rides, it hadn't been an outstanding rodeo. They were used to getting more for their two bucks. A handful, who were seeing their first prison rodeo got up to leave when the rodeo clowns climbed into the fenced pen with the rest of the convicts. The rest waited. Suddenly the center gate swung open and a tall rangy black bull charged into the arena.

It was a cross between the Brahma and the breed of Spanish bull bred especially for the corrida. The Brahma for intelligence and size, the Spanish for wildness, speed, and for horns. This satin black bull's horns curved as long as a man's forearm with the hand outstretched almost straight up from the head. They seemed like two saracen swords guarding the wild brain of the bull which trotted defiantly around the arena, stopping now and then to stare at individual humans in the crowd with eyes an old timer would say could bore right through you. It stopped and stared at Daryl.

Daryl was so amazed by the animal he hadn't noticed that Bones had left his seat along with five other men. The rodeo caller knew the animal held the crowd in thrall and said nothing for a full three minutes. This, after all, was the main event, the real danger. The people wanted blood; they'd get their blood. Then he began to announce in a low voice. "Ladies and gentlemen, you will never see this event in any other rodeo. If you haven't noticed, this bull has a twenty dollar bill rolled up and tied with a rubber band to the ring in its nose. Six convicts will shortly enter the arena with the bull and attempt to grab that twenty dollar bill. These men are serving life sentences and have nothing to lose; (this was usually untrue, but the authorities always thought it would heighten interest in the event) each year we lose a few twenty dollar bills and every so often we lose a convict. That's the risk these boys take on their own accord. No one makes them do it. Since there is a high chance of someone slipping or losing his footage, this bull carries the name of Midnight. It was bred on a ranch in South Texas and never saw a man on foot before. Best to give these boys a big hand when they first come out, for they might not hear you when the event is over. There is a strict twenty minute time limit, and if any contestant is driven to 'tree' by the bull, they can not reenter the contest. They must stay on the ground. And here they are!"

The applause was loud and thunderous. Bones, Moore, Givens, Duckett, Bidwell and Stevens fanned out to face the stomping bull at the far end of the arena. It saw them, did not stop to paw the ground, but charged. It aimed first for Stevens and chased him to the fence; he leaped high onto the boards, but one horn still gouged the calf of his leg. Moore and Bidwell were the next two "treed," Bidwell catching a raking blow from the horns across his back which sent a splash of blood down the back of the white prison shirt which brought a gasp from the crowd. His blood was so hot he felt nothing for a few moments; his attention like everyone else's was riveted on the arena. Givens and Duckett had both worked in past years as rodeo clowns, so they were quicker with eye, hand and foot and could feint and dodge laterally from the bull's charge. Still, they could barely stay out of the way of this Midnight who stood two hands higher than most rodeo bulls and weighed two hundred pounds lighter. Neither had gotten close enough to grab for the twenty dollar bill; they knew that would come only in the last few minutes when and if the bull tired.

Bones looked to be playing a curious role. He was staying almost constantly behind the bull, now and then slapping the bull when it charged Givens and Duckett, the slap introducing an almost imperceptible hesitancy in the bull's charge. Finally the bull ran Duckett to the fence. It might have caught him head on, if Givens had not lunged for the money. The Midnight Bull swung its horns at Givens, its shoulder crashing into Duckett, b reaking a few of his ribs. Duckett climbed painfully out of the arena.

Now it was just Bones and Givens, Bones harrowing the great noble beast from behind and Givens working in closer from the front. Bones hoped Givens would snatch the twenty; he had no use for the money. No, he was here for an older, longer reason. Playing the bull was the only time he felt free, twenty minutes a Sunday, Six Sundays out of the year.

The black bull would whirl trying to catch Bones, but Bones would stay with it, always moving back in behind the bull, so the Midnight had to keep turning its head to see him. Finally, Givens had worked his way in close, close enough to grab for the green paper hanging like a jeweled blade of grass above the froth of the bull's mouth. He misjudged the quickness of the animal though; Bones, guessing quickly the moves of both man and beast, grabbed the tail of Midnight giving it the hardest quickest twist he could. The black head swung high. Givens, eager to reach, stumbled over his own feet, and a half ton of cattle laid its hooves into him.

Bones rode the bull's tail on out into a wide circle giving Givens time to scramble away with only a busted wrist and a nasty cut on the brow. As Bones turned loose the tail he whirled wide to face the bull for the first time. Five minutes were left, and it was one man facing one bull in a timeless ritual of blood and sand.

The mates in the pen started changing: "Bones, Bones, Bones, Bones, Bones, Bones—" They all knew of Bones' Indian blood, though he never spoke of it. Not a few wanted to see some of that blood spilled.

William Bones had not been dropped on the ground by his mother to be killed by a bull. When only ten he would run down jackrabbits on the North Texas plains. He now began a furious, controlled dance that shocked the bull almost as much as the roaring crowd. When the bull charged he would feint, sidestep, and box the bull on the jaw or ears or horns as it swept past. He played the Midnight so close, at times it seemed as if *he* were charging the bull instead.

Minutes passed. The crowd was beside itself. The roar was so constant it hung like a deathly silence; it was just there. No one was conscious of their screaming. Finally Bones grabbed the tiring bull by both horns driving his weight into the neck of the animal, then pivoted on the ball of his right foot as he turned loose with his left hand. His right arm yanked down on the ebony horn as Midnight heaved all its weight into him. Then dancing away, but into the charging black bull, Bones grabbed the brass ring with his left hand, jerking down and back with all his might, then leaping clear of the bull Midnight which crumpled in the dust of its own great weight and strength led by the man's hand on its head.

Bones quickly climbed aloft on the board railing and unrolled the green twenty dollar bill which had come away in his hand. He was no longer in the freedom of the dance. He hated the crowd and hated the money in his hand and how he had gotten it. But he waved it in the air for all to see. That was the rule.

In the arena, the black bull, Midnight, stood defeated, tossing its head wildly for the forked creature that had so shortly before breathed on its nose. The curved ebony above its head no longer looked like Saracen blades; they were simply horns the length of a man's forearm with the hand outstretched.

## Chapter XIX ON THE DOUBLE

The next morning began like all Mondays; the groans at the 5:15 bell, the men herding up for the beans, hoecake of cornbread, and blackstrap molasses breakfast. Navy beans for breakfast, pinto beans for supper, and only in the fields were they allowed to fart.

Bones and Daryl were on the same work detail, fixing a hay mower, then mowing and baling forty acres of prime Johnson grass. The Johnson grass hay would only bring fifty cents a bale in the dead of winter, but it cost Central I almost nothing: gasoline and a few pounds of lube for the machines, and pinto beans to grease the joints of the inmates.

Today, the mower was haywired. Someone had forgotten the lube for a week or ten days, and the blades were stuck to the camshaft, stiff as a board. The ten man crew had just managed to prop the mower up to get at the blades when a rider from the Central rode up. "Warden Shoat wants Bones in his office in twenty minutes. One of you two will have to take him. I've got to get on down to the timber crew in the bottom."

Bones, his face showing no feelings, tensed his body, waiting for the order to move. One of the two mounted guards, Rader started cussing. "Goddamit, Bones. What kind of shit is this. Can't get no work done with you pissing in your pants in the Warden's office. Team up there! Halftrot! Hah!"

Trotting back to the prison with the big Morgan close behind, Bones culled through his head the last two months, trying to figure why he was being called on the carpet. No reason. But their memory was working better than his; *they* had a reason.

As they trotted down the dirt road behind the brick ranch-style homes of the guards, Bones saw a guard's wife hanging out clothes; the wind briefly blew her thin cotton dress flush against her thighs and he felt a strange mixed desire tug hard at his gut. Not desire for her, but desire to be free mingled with an old half-buried memory of the woman he had fought over, the woman who sent him up with her lying words.

"Eyes center, Bones. You got no call to look over there. Double time from here to the gate!"

Hate churned in him so slowly and surely he did not even know any longer that it was hate. The hate was always there like the ocean, occasionally rolling up in a huge wave to flood the waking mind. God, he hated the guards and their squat little brick houses and their squat little wives who bossed the old neutered convicts in clipping their St. Augustine lawns. He hated, too, the way they denuded the live oaks along the drives, leaving only a bare thatch of leaves at the top of the limbless trunk. Those oak trees were in prison, too.

The hate was still washing inside him when he stepped through the doors of the warden's office. Warden Shoat, actually Deputy Warden Shoat since Null was so jealous of his title that he was the only full warden in the state, leaned back and smiled at Bones. He looked closely at the bronze face stretched tautly over the high cheekbones and the hawk's nose. The black eyes were deep wells of forgetfulness that told him nothing. No fear, no resentment, no smirk, and certainly no respect showed. The smile slowly left Shoat's face. "Bones, do you know why you're here?"

"No sir."

"Are you wondering why you're here?"

"Yes sir."

"You know you haven't been *here* very often in your four years at Sugarland, have you?"

"No sir."

"You've kept your nose clean, Bones."

"Yes sir."

"At least, you've tried."

"Yes sir, I've tried."

"Warden Null tells me you put on quite a show in the rodeo up at The Walls in Huntsville yesterday."

Bones merely nodded.

"Where did you learn that much about cattle."

"As a boy, sir. I worked on the remnants of the old XIT ranch on the plains, then for a few years on what's now the Baugh place at Double Mountain. Later I drifted to Alpine to work that big herd of Longhorns and that's where I got into the trouble that brought me here."

"A lot of men work cattle, Bones. But you know more than most. How come?"

"Well, sir. I'm not sure I can answer that. It was just that I and my brother, as boys, we would ride every animal on the place, cows, bulls, horses, mules, jacks. Well, sometimes we rode them, and sometimes they rode us."

"Ha! Ha! Haw! Go on, Bones. Tell me some more."

"Yes sir. I reckon the main thing about all this riding is that you lose all your fear of the animal. You come to know the way its mind works, and you no longer fear it."

"What led you to work those longhorns?"

"Well, they're smarter and wilier than any other cattle. They've gone back to the wild. They were so wild the owner, Kilpatrick, couldn't even catch the calves to brand them. The old ones had retired on him; he needed a cowhand, so he hired me."

"Did you ever ride a longhorn?"

Bones looked at him straight. "Yes sir."

Shoat stirred in his seat. Not quite conscious of it, he felt he was learning almost too much about this Bones. It was said that Bones had never shown fear to a guard; if that were so, then Bones was to be feared. Shoat felt, too, the one instant when Bones' black eyes bored into him, that Bones had robbed him of a knowledge of himself he was not even sure he had.

"Well, let's get to the point. I've got a lot of work piled up. Warden Null wants a critique of the rodeo from you. We want to make it better, spruce it up. It's a long way from Dallas and we want to give those people their money's worth. He said some of the rodeo was slow."

"Yes sir. Every year I've been here, it's always started slow. I reckon that's because the work schedule stiffens us up, and we don't hit our stride until the third or fourth rodeo."

"Any ideas how we can change that?"

"Yes sir. Repeat the best performances in the rodeo."

"You mean, give them more than one start out the gate."

"Yes sir." Bones' mind was churning now, as fast as his legs churned the day before in front of the bull called Midnight. "There's something else you might consider, too."

"What's that?"

"There was only one performance among the regular events that was a show-stopper."

"Yeh, I know. Connors' calf-roping. What of it?"

"Well, sir. Calf-roping is a lot chancier than the other events. Besides giving Connors two starts out of the gate, if you let him practice roping during the week, he'll give you a show-stopper every time he's up."

"I wouldn't interfere with his work schedule."

"No sir. I mean, let him practice in the mornings real early before his work schedule starts."

"I see. Just where do you think we could let him practice."

"The pasture by Milburn Road is fenced. Keep his horse there, and there's a shed for his saddle and ropes."

"Well, we'll see what we can do about that. Any other ideas?"

"Yes sir. The ones who are signed up for bull and bronc riding. Give them a half day off on Saturday and they'll give you a better ride on Sunday."

"That will be harder to do, but we might try it for a week or two. That'll be all, Bones. You can go now." Shoat's fat, uncalloused hands shuffled at the papers on his desk; he could not quite bring his eyes back up to look at Bones.

While Bones was threading his way through the warden's thicket, the work crew had finally wrenched the blade loose on the mower. Daryl had a hold on the blade with his left hand, and when it gave without warning, the blade sheared into his left index finger against the blade guard.

Daryl yelled to hold it. With his right hand he rolled the blade up to where he could extract his left. The finger dangled, spurting blood; only the skin and a bit of flesh held it on.

Daryl's only thought was to stanch the bleeding. No amount of pressure on the finger stopped it; it bled like a stuck pig. He only heard the guard cursing him; he did not see the leather quirt swung fiercely at his head. Luckily, after it landed, he was blinded with rage and could not see the guard; else, he might have swung at him with his good, but blood-soaked right hand.

The guard shouted at the work crew. I'm running him to the shed. Any of you rabbit, you'll be shot down. Now run, you bloody bastard, run!"

Halfway to the infirmary, after a good quarter mile, they crossed Rader and Bones heading back. Daryl sucked in his breath for an instant as his guard yelled, "Rader, get down there quick. Those shithooks are loafing on us."

At the infirmary they sewed Daryl's finger back on. "Lucky that cut was at the joint. Otherwise, we would have had to take your finger off."

They left the nerve balled up on the side of the finger, however, and the dull ache of it on rainy cold days would leave the memory of that day forever livid in his mind.

## Chapter XX RIDING A PAINT HORSE TO VICTORY

The cell door unbolted. Connors raised his head from his bunk. Still pitch dark. "What's up, boss? I ain't done nothing."

"It ain't what you did; it's what you're gonna do. Get your work clothes on, Connors. We got work for you."

"Yes suh, boss. Gimme one minute more 'n I'm yours."

Connors was still rubbing the sleep from his eyes as he trotted in the pre-dawn dark in front of the mounted guard. When they came to the gate of the high-fenced pasture, they were met by another guard leading a paint horse, saddled, with two lariats slung over the horn. Inklings jelled; Connors' face split into a wide grin, his teeth an ivory white in the gray light of dawn.

"Boss, you gonna let me ride this hoss."

"That's right, boy. You're gonna ride and rope for the next two hours. Then you join up the work crew baling hay. One of their guards will come unlock this gate and let you out. Unsaddle your horse when you're done and tether it with one of your ropes, so you can catch it easy the next morning. Leave the saddle and blanket in the shed."

"Boss, who done me this favor."

"They say Bones put in a word for you with the warden. Seems like you and him's the big rodeo stars."

"A star! Not me, boss. I is just a nigguh!"

"Ha! Ha! That's right, Connors. You is just a nigger. Okay, lock him up in there. Get to roping, nigger."

Then the guards were gone. Bones was alone with the paint horse. He swung easily up into the saddle and hefted one of the hemp ropes in his hand. He loosened the noose and twirled it fancifully over his head as he trotted the pony out towards the middle of the field. Pleasure coursed through every pore of his body. Having the horse between his legs was almost as good as having a woman there.

"No guards. I'm holding jiggers for myself. Whoop! Whoop! Get on there, pony. Let's see you jump that twelve-foot fence."

Connors slowly practiced the rope, tossing it out on the run, then drawing it back in as he stopped and wheeled the horse. He did this semi-consciously; while his eye studied the whole lay of the land. On the far side of the pasture was the Milburn road. If he could just get word out to Truck and Bennie. His mind flashed on it. That's it. The hound dog man. There's my ticket ———.

That night after supper the mates were lounging in the *ball park;* a few listened to their radios, some strummed their beat-up four-string guitars. About eight o'clock, Connors spoke to the *bull* policing the pen: "Walkin' my dog here, boss."

"Okay, Connors, walk your dog."

Walking the dog meant the inmate could leave the compound and walk to the fifty foot high, electrified, chain-link fence and take a leak. There was the only contact the prisoners had with the outside world besides Sunday visitors. One convict slept outside the prison.

Abercrombie, the hound dog man, slept in the shed with four bloodhounds. He fed and trained the hounds, kept them from barking at night, and ran a few hundred illicit chores for the guards and the prisoners. Late at night he would sneak off to the town of Sugarland, and in the shadow of the Imperial sugar elevators, buy dope for inmates who had passed him the money. Usually it was chewing tobacco laced with cocaine. Lucrative because a little *coke* went a long way. The trouble with Crumb, as he was called, was his deafness in one ear. He'd only come to the fence when he heard someone pissing. Naturally, he who could piss the loudest and longest could get his attention more often than not.

Connors had been saving up all day; his bladder was full to bursting. He looked up at the tower forty yards away. No guard in sight; he must be up there whacking off over some two-bit Fawcett novel. Connors unlimbered his tallywhacker and cut loose with a mighty stream.

In a moment Crumb shuffled up out of the shadows.

"Oh, it's you, Connors. It sounded like a cow pissing on a flat rock. I swear I was about off to sleep, but you shore woke me up."

"Crumb, how is you, man?"

"I'm fine now that summer's come. Warm weather and my rheumatism always eases up. One of my dogs is ailing though. Just a touch of mange. I've been treating her with creosote. Dunno where she picked it up."

"Reckon she caught it from one of these mangy guards?"

"Heh. Heh. Yeh, sure enough. That's were it's coming from. What's on your mind, Connors?"

"I've got a hanker for some of that special Abercrombie chewing tobacco."

"Taken up the habit, have you?"

"No habit. Just a little taste. Bet you use some, don't you?"

"No, I never touch the stuff. I stick to my sun-cured Bloodhound store-bought plug. But I don't blame a feller for wanting a little something extra. Anything that helps you make it through the work schedule or through the night for that matter. Pass me the bread real careful; that double wire is full of juice."

"Here's twelve smackers. A ten and two singles. How much tobacco will that get me?"

"Oh, about half a pound. But it's real strong stuff, got a kick like a mule. If you don't chew it but just kinda suck on it, one little chaw will last all day."

"And maybe you could mail this letter for me."

"Who's it to?"

"My sugar down in Louisiana. They won't allow us to write through normal channels."

"Ha. Ha. I see. I can make it out. Benna Glaspar, Burr Oak Barbecue, Monroe, Louisiana. Some of that Cajun poontang, huh."

"Yessuh. And she is mellow. I'm just telling her to keep the fire hot."

"Okay, Connors. It'll be in the mail tonight. Tomorrow night you get your tobacco."

"Thank you, mister hound dog boss. I'm much obliged."

"Think nothing of it, Connors. It's my pleasure. So long."

"So long." Connors turned back towards the north wing of the compound.

Abercrombie stepped into the shed to copy down the address in his secret ledger. Should something come of this, an escape maybe, that address would be worth some money—at least fifty dollars—to a certain guard. He, in turn, would sell it for a hundred to the warden. "Benna! I'll bet she's a pretty, big-titted nigger." Abercrombie fiddled his flesh through his trousers. "Connors is sending her a little sugar from Sugarland.

By the midnight mail. I'll just tuck it in here next to my heart so it will keep warm on the way to town. Might make it sweeter for some white man's heat to be on the letter. Sweets for the sweet. Twelve dollars. That's sure some sugar in the pot. . . ."

* * *

That week Connors got close enough to Bones just one time to talk to him, and then only for a brief moment. Under the watchful eyes of the guards, whole life histories would be condensed and spoken in a few moments.

"How does that paint horse ride?"

"She dances and spins like a top. She's so much fun I may just skip that next rodeo and stay down here to ride my horse."

"Gonna hang up your bit and the bosses' spurs?"

"For keeps. Yourself?"

"Before the first frost, while the Brazos is still warm."

"Well, look me up. I'm owing you a favor."

"When?"

"When you get to New Orleans."

"They say the old Mississip is deep and wide."

"Ha! Ha! Git along, Bones. I can't keep up wid you. I'm gonna be gone like a turkey through the corn with his long johns on and you'll be left here to hold jiggers for me.

* * *

Friday morning, 3:30, Connors is pulling on his britches when the *bull* unlocks his cell. Unhurriedly, he hurries through the ritual talk and gestures till he's astride his paint horse in the pasture. Once astride that pony, he slouches like one of the pagan gods who has all the time in the world. He keeps sidling the horse next to the fence away from the Milburn Road. No guards are in sight; the one who herded him down here has already tumbled back into his sack.

From up the road comes the faint, familiar sputter of a pickup truck. Connors right hand moves excitedly as he leans forward and spurs the paint in a beeline for the other fence. He no longer hears the motor. "What's wrong? He's coastin'. Truck's coastin' on in."

The pony snorts as he's hauled up short at the fence. Truck's already out with the wire cutters and Benna's sitting in the front seat waving her red scarf at him. No one says a word.

Truck cuts the wire as high as he can reach then peels back about a five foot strip of the chain-link fence. Connors backs the pony up to get a run: there's a six foot deep barditch to jump once he's through the fence.

Truck is already back in the truck with his hand on the starter. Then Connors, his grin splitting his dark face, rides hard and low for the hole in the fence which he hardly sees in the dark.

The pony is skittish, but trusts the firm directions of the easy rider on her back. As she scrapes through the opening, the horse and rider arc together as one flesh in the leap over the barditch. Her front hooves catch and she climbs up onto the dirt road. Benna motions him toward the trailer, but Connors is ahead of her. He knows, and rides the horse right on up into the covered horse trailer, then clambers down and pulls up the gate behind him.

Truck starts the motor and eases the pickup and trailer off to the north towards Milburn. Connors knows but knows not the joy that surges through him. He has rode his Paint Horse to Victory.

Freedom and the sweet arms of Benna will be his when they cross the Bon Wier and hit that Louisiana line. . . .

## Chapter XXI THE CANNERY

Connors' escape put Bones and a dozen others on the shitlist. Bones, specifically, was forbidden to participate in or even watch prison rodeos the rest of the summer. A state-wide dragnet was thrown up when Connors was found gone, but to no avail; several dozen cars and pickups of black farmers were redlighted over to the side in the deep piney woods of east Texas and blustery highway patrolmen and sheriffs poked through old blankets on the floorboards and opened trunks, but Connors was long gone just like *a turkey through the corn.*

The whole work crew that Bones had been on, baling hay, were shifted en masse to the hellhole of the prison; the twelve hour shift in the Cannery. Impossible to sleep during the day with the harsh lights, the clanging iron doors, and the radios, Daryl found his strength and will sapped by the mind-numbing pace of the cannery. At The Walls, the convicts were doing equally mindless work making license plates and running the jute mill. The jute mill was comparable to the cannery; there the fibers bit into the nose and lungs and the noise deafened the ears. The okra and tomatoes were the main products at the cannery, though field corn, too, could be had for the shucking. Try shucking five thousand ears of corn in a twelve hour shift—standing up, feet still, hands and arms shucking and flying—six nights a week.

Daryl got stuck on the tomato line. With a tiny dull paring knife he grabbed the boiling hot tomatoes as they tumbled from the scalding water onto the conveyor belt, reamed the stems at the top and pitched them in the pot. Six men on both sides of the belt rooted to the spot, hands working like bees, sweat pouring from their heads like horses' sweat. No thoughts could persist before the relentless stream of fiery red tomatoes rolling down the belt. The hands blistered, the blisters popped, annealed, and new blisters gathered under the old blisters. No gloves were issued for indoor work.

The *bulls* kept a lot of pressure on to boot. No distance separated them and their wormy contempt for the inmates. Here they weren't on horseback but right behind one's shoulder, shouting in the ear. Daryl thought sure he'd see a stabbing his fifth night on the line. One of the most hated *bulls* was a huge thick-jowled man they called Major. He may once have been a major in some fool's army, or a major domo, or a drum corps major. Whatever, inside Sugarland, his was a Major act.

In the fields he was noted for lashing with his quirt right across the heads of workers when they least expected it and muttering some such bull as "Nipped that daydream in the bud. Now you all get back to work."

Inside the cannery, his harsh gravelly voice was the lash. Forbidden to talk most of the work time, the ears of a prisoner become as sensitive as raw sores; they seek out the deafening roar of machines to dull their accountability to the curses and insults of the guards. The major's voice always cut through this veneer of solitude like a hacksaw.

On Daryl's fifth night in this frenzy, he noticed a slender young red-haired kid from Houston—sent up on his second auto theft—was about to give out midway through the shift. The irony lay in the fact that if he collapsed on the line, he would more likely be thrown into the Hole first, then the Hospital. The threat of this punishment kept convicts chained as if by shackles to the steady grueling grind of the workline. If one's hand is held to the grindstone and is being eaten away by the carborundum, a man will do all in his might to jerk the hand away, or pass out from the pain. However, if one's whole being–mind, blood, flesh and bone–is forced to the grindstone, and the inner will itself is perverted into reinforcing the bond–a will pulled by the fear of the unknown that follows a refusal to perform–then being itself palls into non-being; the will, identity and health destroyed, and how great must be that destruction. To live in this prison, driven like mules, denounced like dogs, those alone can keep their humanity who steel their memory to remember the beauty of the freedom of their childhood. For those doomed to forget that period when they moved in the world like a young wild deer, the godlight would flicker and go out in their eyes. Terrible it is to see these dull-eyed men. The guards were largely dull-eyed. The young guards would avert their eyes until they either quit the job or grew into the shape of men like the major. For many of the guards, the *benefits:* the free houses, medical care, free vegetables, free convict labor to mow the lawns, water the roses, feed the horses and prune the trees, was what held them to the job; like the military, only gratuities could hold them to a system they didn't believe in until the ice-cold morning arose when they saw it all as necessity.

So, on the fifth night out, Daryl's pain was paradoxically forgotten as his attention riveted on the greater pain inflicting the red-headed inmate across the conveyor belt. Three, four times, the Major walked by, saw Red faltering, leaned and shouted in his ear. The words were inaudible to Daryl in the din, but he saw Red stiffen and his hands jerk like a puppets'–pulled by unseen strings connected to nerve and sinew—and plow again into the steaming flow of scalding tomatoes.

On the fifth time the Major said nothing but reached a fat paw into the tomatoes and popped/smeared the wet red flame in Red's face. Red's white fingers that gripped the paring knife turned ash-white then livid. Daryl knew his will had turned. But the stab of the arm never came; there was no longer enough strength for that, and even if he could have swung his fist clenching the knife for the Major's heart, the dull penknife would have had the tough khaki shirt to tear through and beneath that the Major's tough hide and inches of fat and muscle and bone protecting the heart, and if the knife can't cut through to the black heart, why stab at all.

So, on the fifth night out, Red was saved by his weakness from having twenty years stuck onto his two year sentence for murderous assault on a guard. Come morning, at breakfast, Daryl sat by him and whispered, "Put in a chit to transfer back to The Walls. At least there, they'll put you on dayshift and you can get some sleep at night." Red merely nodded. But he put in the chit and maybe to prove that there are some few mild, scattered remnants of justice in the universe, his chit was approved. Daryl never knew whether he did his time or not.

*Small wonder then,* when the convicts could see the thousands upon hundreds of thousands of cans of vegetables they packed day and night, and saw the name brand trucks that loaded up the cans to haul them to a Houston warehouse where nicely printed, clean, respectable labels were placed on the cans before they made their way to the supermarket shelf, where unknowing housewives would buy them gladly clucking to themselves, "what a bargain: tomatoes only 37 cents a can," the inmates *knowing* how many hundreds of thousands of dollars that lined the pockets of the prison system and bought the new Chevrolet sedans every year for the upper level officials and bought every last ounce of their gasoline, and perpetuated the need for a great pool of unskilled convict labor to keep this profitable machine running at the outrageous cost of 10 cents per man per day, the lying prison officials telling the state legislature every year that while the maintenance of the prison and the feeding of the prisoners were paid by the prison profits, they would still need a few million dollars for capital improvement for more prison buildings since the overall prison population was rising faster percentage-wise than the population of Texas, and the average length of terms for all offenses had increased twenty percent in the last ten years and the rate of recidivism since World War II had grown from 50% to 80%, *small wonder then,* that the convicts embittered by the toil and by the knowledge of the vast profits of this slave system should try to add a dose of convict spit to every can of tomatoes, okra, and corn they could, even whip a stream of convict piss now and again into the steaming vats of vegetables, even on rare occasion strain and strain at the workline and shit their pants and when the guards had passed—dart a hand into their pants to fling the turds into the tomatoes a-canning—hot, wet tomatoes to clean the shit from the hand—and the peaceful unsuspecting citizens sitting down to their meals all over the nation, opening their name-brand cans of vegetables, and sometimes wondering but never knowing why the canned okra seemed extra slick or why there were yellow or brown streaks in the red tomatoes or why the corn tasted funny.

*"Convict spit or convict shit in every can" was the watchword at the Cannery.* The guards, too, trapped in the same prison, would often spit a lunger into the vast swirling vats.

## Chapter XXII COTTON PICKING

Years later when Daryl set these words down he did not remember much more about the five weeks spent in the cannery twelve hours a night except the red-hot tomato smeared in Red's face and that it was five weeks of living hell.

In September Daryl's folks came to see him again, his mother with a basket full of homemade oatmeal cookies. His father looked much older than Daryl could have imagined, but when he thrust his hand into that large rough hand that had pushed a mule-pulled plough for forty years, the grip told him his Dad was okay.

"This place has put some steel in your grip, son."

"I wouldn't have known that, Dad. It still seems like every day's work could be my last."

"Don't talk that way before your Mama. She's been circulating a petition to get you home early on parole."

"That won't do no good."

"How do we know what good it will do until we've tried it?" His mom's jaw was set. "I'll have you know that every woman in the Ladies Bible Class signed, even Miz McElmore, and I only had to quote one scripture on them. "When I was in jail and you visited me; when I was sick and you ministered unto me." So, we are doing all we can to get you out."

"I know, I know. Don't get upset. It's just that the cotton season is here, and the word is—they don't allow no paroles in pickin' time, cause they got to get the cotton in."

"Well, that beats all I ever heard. Just wait till the judge hears about that."

"Aw, Mom. Here, let me hug your neck. I've got to go soon. I'll be all right. They been working us awful hard, but they ain't broke my spirit yet."

"They couldn't do that son. Not to a Barnes." The eyes of the two men caught and held. Daryl felt his father's will flow into him like a flood of old memory; he suddenly knew that will had been flowing into him all summer and he had been barely aware of it.

"Next time we come, it'll be to take you home."

"Maybe Christmas."

"You leave that up to the Lord."

They embraced again, then parted. Daryl watched them walk away, his mother in her homemade calico, his father in his Dickie's khaki pants and long-sleeved shirt, his broad shoulders slightly slumped by the heavy prison air.

Then the cotton was upon them.

Daryl had picked a lot of cotton for nineteen going on twenty. Every fall after school let out, and all day Saturday, he picked, out of necessity, and to help his neighbors, the Vaughans, Umphress, and Ables, get their crop in. While they kept saying the machines were coming, so far they hadn't crept up the Brazos Valley. Daryl hoped they never would.

The old saying: "All it takes to pick cotton is a strong back and a weak mind." At Sugarland all it took was a strong back.

Daryl had never picked more than 275 pounds in one day. Driven to the fields at daybreak and picking until it was too dark to see the white cotton curling from the bolls, with mounted guards like the Major pushing them down the rows, Daryl hit 450 pounds his first day and never went below that. Bones stunned Daryl by picking over 600 a day and up to 800 as the season wore on and the bolls opened fully. Somebody told him Leadbelly, back in the twenties, picked a thousand pounds a day on a few occasions, and that when stupid newspaper reporters would ask him if that were true, Led would say, "Course it's true. I don't need to say somethin' that's not true. Course, to do that, ya got to really jump around!" Daryl learned fast how to really jump around that cotton patch. As Bones told him, "It's both a fight and a flow. The less thinking you do, the more energy that can flow into the hand and eye. If you're picking out ahead of the pack, you won't have a guard on your back. Now that will interrupt your flow sure enough."

"You got to just do the cotton as quick as you can, and remember that it's just another way of passing time. The only thing you'll know when the cotton's in—and every last boll gets picked on this place—is whether or not your back's broke, and if it ain't broke, you're all right. Every year it takes me two or three weeks after pickin's done to regain my equilibrium."

Except for a few nooks and crannies of freshly cleared ground near the river bottom, the rows of cotton on the flat coastal plain seemed to stretch endlessly in length. After each weigh-up, the wagons would move another three hundred yards up the field and then wait, their slats grinning, for the pickers to catch up. The purpose of the long rows—Daryl thought—was to make the prisoners think they could never finish them out, and even when they did turn a row, the sheer infinity of the new row overwhelmed the brief flash of joy felt at finishing the old one. As Bones said, there's no satisfaction till the crop's all in, and you're still alive.

The cannery had shut down and all two thousand mates were toting a sack. Evidently cotton was the big money crop. Daryl was good in math; the numbers would rattle through his head. "Let's see: 2,000 pickers a day averaging 400 pounds each is 800,000 pounds a day, which—baled out—will be a thousand bales a day for at least forty days. Forty Thousand bales, no it can't be quite that much. There's eight thousand acres and even with all this rain and sun they don't get much more than three bales an acre, so that's twenty-four thousand bales, baled out. It must taper off the last couple of weeks. So, 24,000 bales at $120 a bale gives twice 144 or 288 thousand, no, two million eight hundred and eighty thousand dollars just off the cotton crop. 2,000 men a day at 10 cents a day is 200 dollars a day times 40 days is 8,000 dollars for the labor picking it. Whew! That's a pile of money for somebody's pocket. At times Daryl's figuring would be slashed open by the Major's long quirt laid across his back. "Hah! Caught you napping, asswipe! This ain't no Sunday School. Pick it on out!"

Goddamn right it ain't no Sunday School.

Daryl remembered when as a little boy his mama had made his first knee patches and he had followed his father and brothers into the fields, the cotton stalks as high as his head, the sandy soil pushing and squishing between his toes, the occasional bull nettle or red ant which would sting him and his father's spittle of tobacco juice which always cooled the sting. Then it was a pleasure to pluck the cotton from the boll, the fibered fur like white puffs of spun gold, made of earth and air. Here, he never had that sensation, that give of the cotton in his paw; it moved too quickly from stalk to sack, his hands but steel brushes on the generator. The words from an old Bob Wills song kept running in his mind:

*Little bee sucks the blossom,*
*Big bee eats the honey;*
*Little man picks the cotton,*
*Big man gets the money. . . .*

At night his bones could not straighten out in time, so he slept on his side. He knew now how old man Grant, the grave-digger, had got so stooped. Sometimes, there was a boll of cotton in his dream, but he could not get ahold of it. He would reach out for it, maybe fancy he touched it, but he could not feel it give.

## Chapter XXIII OUT ON PAROLE

Daryl did not last the season. His mother was right about a few things, and this was one of them. She hadn't minced words with the judge; she said simply, "They're working him to death down there, your honor, and I need him home. Here's over three hundred people in town that attest to his character.

"I understand your feelings, Mrs. Barnes. I'll be glad to pass this on to the parole board. I can only make a recommendation, but I'll be glad to do that."

It must have been strongly put, for the parole board passed Daryl's application and let him out in the middle of pickin' time. Not quite ten months of hard time. Ten months of hard labor. Where had it gone to?

The day before he was due to get out Daryl sat by Bones at supper. Not much was said. Bones would mutter sternly, "Your next year will be as hard as this one. The local law will worry you every way it can to get you sent back here. But you'll make it."

"If you ever get out of here, Bones, you know you're welcome at our house."

"Thanks. I'm obliged. I may just leave this place soon, but if I do, I'll probably take a trip south. I'll drop you a line though to let you know how I'm faring."

"I'd appreciate it. I don't reckon I'd have made it if you hadn't shown me the ropes."

"You'd have made it. You might have taken a few more lumps, but you'd have made it."

"One thing I'll never forget."

"Eh?"

"That day you locked horns with old Midnight."

The faintest smile played across Bones' face like a butterfly dancing in the breeze. Beneath the stern exterior, the kindness of the man gleamed for an instant. "Yes, I'll remember Midnight, too. Remember well—."

"Take care of yourself, Bones."

"You take care, Daryl. I don't want to hear of you getting into trouble."

"No sir. I won't. You can hold jiggers I won't."

The next day dragged mercilessly. The manner of the prison's outgoing indoctrination told Daryl much about the cast of mind of the guards. All his property was inventoried; he was missing a toothbrush. The cost of the 39 cent toothbrush came out of his accumulated fund.

When the prison guard was explaining the conditions of his parole he began to have flashes of doubt that they would really let him go, or that his folks would be waiting for him. "Barnes, I don't need to tell you that most people, once they been in, can't make it on the outside. Most of them bust their parole in a week or a month. Did you know that?"

"No sir."

"If you're going to make your parole, you'll know that the minute you step outside these gates. You'll know whether or not you'll go straight. Do you know what *go straight* means?"

"Yes sir."

"Well, Barnes, I give you maybe nine months on the

outside before you'll be back. That's the longest first offenders can stay on the outside before they're back inside the walls. Nine months is the maximum. Now follow me."

Daryl followed the guard through the halls of the administration building, four paces back, as he's been trained. His eyes riveted on the military crease of the guard's khakis and how it crinkled each step the guard took. *Crinkle.* Straight. *Crinkle.* Straight. *Crinkle.* Straight. *Crinkle.*

Then they were at the door, and the guard or deputy, deputy warden: this deputy of the deputies: ran his last number on Daryl. "Here are your release papers, and the address of your parole officer. You must contact him immediately upon reaching home. Immediately! Is that clear?"

Daryl was bound and determined that not one more *yessir* or *nosir* would cross his lips, so he just nodded.

"Now, you march up to that electric gate and stand at attention. When I hit the buzzer from inside the office, they'll open the first gate. You march forward and stand at attention until they close that gate and open the outer gate. You make one false move, and the guards in the tower will shoot you. You're mighty lucky getting out in the middle of cotton picking. Somebody pulled some strings for you. Just file this away in your head. Somebody can pull some strings to get you back in here, too. Now take your walking papers and shove off."

As Daryl marched up to the first thirty foot gate he saw the guard in the tower flash his Thompson machine gun, and he flashed back on when he first saw those guns at *The Walls* in Huntsville. The snouts of the guns were ugly as death. He guessed that was part of their job: to flash the Thompson at him one last time. He wondered if it was written down on a rule sheet: "Show weapons to prisoner before opening the gate."

The electric gate opened. He stepped through to the outer prison yard. The gate slammed shut behind him. After an interminable fifty seconds the gate in front of him opened. His knees felt like rubber. Walking out the fast gate, they almost gave out. Then there was the asphalt parking lot and the familiar square roof of the old black Chevrolet. Daryl tried to fight back the tears, but quit when he saw it was no use.

His Daddy wrapped him in a bear hug and his mother rained kisses on him. Finally he was embarrassed by the affection and said, "Let's go home." On the way back he sat on the front seat between them. There was something uncannily strange about these two people who had begot him out of their blood; the flood of their warmth and love and the unsearchable familiarity of their faces seemed passing strange to Daryl after the straits of Sugarland.

All the way home his father spoke hardly a word. His mother alternated between spells of silence and spells of telling him everything that had happened since he'd been gone. "Old man Fitzgerald died. The sheriff came and found him in his cellar after someone complained they hadn't seen him in a long while. He'd been dead three weeks. Which goes to show that living or dead, most people take no mind of you. Grady Harris says you can go to work at his filling station. It's not much, but it's a dollar quarter an hour and it's full time. That little waitress at the cafe, what's her name, Faye? asked about you. She asked when you were coming home. I told her we might bring you back this trip."

As they neared the courthouse square of his hometown on the Brazos, Daryl's father cleared his throat and said, "I reckon it was rough down there, weren't it, Son."

"Yep. It was rough."

Then they were wheeling into the square; the late evening sun had turned the white limestone of the high old courthouse into a shade of fine gold. The tide of simultaneous strangeness and familiarity washed over Daryl. He knew he had a knowledge now of himself and of the world that had nothing to do with this little town and those peaceful stones gleaming yellow in the sun.

His folks stirred comfortably beside him. Then they were crossing the tracks and climbing the hill past the North Side grocery up past the graveyard and the water tower, then out the Cedar Bluff Road towards home.

## Chapter XXIV STRUCK BY LIGHTNING

*"Every beast is driven to the fields with a blow."*

Mid-October saw the cotton two-thirds picked. In the sweltering heat many of the younger mates dropped like flies and would be dragged off to the middle of the road, sometimes staggering back to their feet and fumbling into their cotton sack, sometimes hauled like cordwood back to the infirmary, stuffed there with drugs and back to the fields in two days. Only seldom would a bit of wind swing up from the gulf with a scent of rain to cool the rivers of sweat that poured from every scalp. Even the guards, sitting the backs of the big morgans, carried three or four kerchiefs to mop the sweat from under the brim of their straw hats. Their fingers never strayed for long from the grip of the Winchester and Marlin 30-30's, however; cotton time was the season of most escapes and attempteds. The Major was cruel as ever; his long braided black leather crop kept whistling on backs.

Ever since Connors had busted out, Bones had found his itch to escape from the foul hell of Sugarland was biting deeper into the back of his mind. Now, Barnes was on parole. Bones knew why he had taken a liking to Daryl; the quiet stoicism had reminded him too much of himself at that age.

The cotton flew under his hand. Four weighings in the morning, three this evening, at eighty pounds apiece meant 560 pounds of cotton, not quite a bale when ginned. Bones reflected that on the outside picked cotton would bring three dollars a hundred, but here on this infernal farm, only six months pay added up to fifteen dollars. Connors got a horse thrown in to boot. Bones would settle for just his hide.

He was picking out ahead of everyone, yet with the turn of the sack as he swung back and forth between the two rows, he saw all that happened in the field. The guards as always hung back to haze the stragglers. Only the Major rode all over the field, slowing his yellow mare, an American Saddle breed, to walk quietly up the sandy rows until he could quirt his crop down the straining back of a cotton picker. He and three other guards were hazing the fifty mates on this side of the enormous field, and the trusty, old and brittle, was left to drive the cattle truck that hauled the convicts and pulled the cotton trailer to and from the fields.

Today the humidity was so high Bones could hardly tell if he was sweating or if the water in the air was simply sticking to him as he moved down the row. A wind stiffened up from the gulf, but did no good; in the packed and stifled air there was no room for the human sweat to go.

Bones kept glancing off to the south towards the Gulf of Mexico, or the Gulf of Ensenada as they called it in the old days. Ensenada for the small bays and coves that various hurricanes had bitten out of the coast over the ages. The rows ran west and the deep Brazos river flowed less than a half mile ahead. Bones knew though that he could never outrun the big Morgans, who stood 14 hands high, to the river, and he didn't relish the notion of a 30-30 slug chewing up his spine. Nope, he needed a little help from the fates and the immutable sky. Today looked like the day it might arrive.

By five o'clock every man in the field was eyeing the sky. The clouds that had boiled up were a deep blue-black; it appeared like the ocean, itself, hovered overhead. Sane men would have already made for cover from the storm that was about to burst. Not so the major. No god-begotten storm was cutting into the work time of his cotton picking crew.

Then the rain fell. Like lead pellets out of the sky that exploded into a splotch of water when they struck the skin. Rain by the buckets full. Worse yet; a dozen stalks of streaked lightning could be seen walking towards them about a mile off to the south. Even the major quailed before this sight of the storm god's blazing yellow fingers scratching out of the sky. His greed, though, for he had a share in the cotton, was still uppermost; he sang out, "Dump your sacks!", his gravel voice somehow cutting through the rising clamor of the storm. All the mates struck the field and bolted like lightning for the trailer and the safety of the rubber-wheeled truck.

Chaos ruled the scene. Bones, the furthest off, imperceptibly lagged on the way to the trailer; his cotton sack was full. The horses were churning. The Major's arm flailed out blindly, striking now horses, now men, now the wet slats of the cotton trailer; an old memory of Guadalcanal, where a sniper's bullet cut a groove for a steel plate in his skull, flashed and chewed like lightning in his brain. Full and half-full cotton sacks were flying up over and into the trailer with dull thuds. The men, soaked to the bone, were piling into the truck.

Then the lightning struck.

Givens, who had felt the Major's lash thrice that day, had only a moment before uttered his barest thought, more to himself than to the other mates in the truck. "I wish to god, lightning would strike him dead." *Him,* the Major.

So when the lightning struck, it was no longer even remarkable that Givens had said what he did, nor remarkable at all that the lightning had struck at all, or that it hit where it did. Afterwards they would say that Givens had called it down, but inwardly would know and recall the forks of lightning stabbing all around, and know that it was only the Stream of Fate men call weird that struck the Major down.

The blue ball of light, the blue blaze, filled the air with its crackle, the eye with its flash as it struck down hitting the Major where his butt met the horse's back. He pitched from the dying horse, a foot snagged in the stirrup. Living but never walking or talking again, he would live out his days as a vegetable, cut and canned by the blaze of lightning that wreaked from the sky.

The guard nearest the Major was knocked half out of his saddle and lost grip of the reins. The mare, given its head, pitchforked around towards the front of the truck. The other two guards leaped down to cut the Major loose. Bones saw his chance.

Keeping the cotton sack slung over his shoulder, he rolled over the high slat of the cotton trailer as if the ground itself had flung him up there. The two tail-enders, Jacobson and Flores, saw what was happening and slung their cotton sacks over on top of Bones; he was already burrowing deep into the cotton pit.

The guards had wrestled the Major up over the horn of a saddle and the two were going to ride him in on their horses. One guard was left to slam the padlock on the cattle truck and ride shotgun alongside. No one called for a head count.

The loaded cattle truck pulling the trailer lumbered to a crawl in the wet sand; then the old trusty shifted to second and headed on west for the river road and the way out. Bones knew, when they started to move, he had not been missed.

From the sound of the horse on the left side of the trailer, Bones guessed what had happened. He figured that when the truck and trailer first swung onto the river road, with the deep bar ditch on the other side, he would make his move.

He crawled cautiously out of the cotton until he lay barely covered; only his high forehead, hawk nose, and blacksnake eyes lifted and rolled back and forth in the driving rain to scan the scene. The two guards toting the major were already lost from sight in the steady downpour.

The heavy truck began its swing out of the field and onto the narrow dirt road. Bones braced himself. As the trailer slid out onto the graveled roadbed, he lifted himself and rolled out over the slats as lightly as he rolled in. Running feet hitting the ground, he swung to the right rear of the trailer pushing it still wider on its arc.

At the pivot of the turn he gave a mighty lateral heave that sent the trailer's right wheels sliding into the ditch. The heavy drag of the axle hitting the ground slowed the slow-moving truck. The guard, a young kid named Durkee just back from a hitch in the Marine Corps where the only notable thing he did was invade Lebanon, spun his horse around. Bones was way ahead of him, circling behind the mare, on its blind side.

He grabbed the reins and the mare's left ear and tugged them down, throwing his weight towards the ground. Many a wild pony he'd thrown in this fashion. Durkee matched the mare's scream as he pitched on his face in the mud. Bones snatched the rifle from its scabbard before the horse regained its feet, and swung it deliberately in a slow heavy arc to deliver a sure and merciful blow to Durkee's head with the butt. Durkee's moan stopped as night spread through his limp body sprawled in the mud.

The old trusty had killed the motor and sat watching the drama through the rain-streaked sideview mirror. The time it took to take place was no more than two minutes, but easily seemed a quarter hour since the weight of going free hung in the balance. Bones swung open the door of the truck, "Hop out, old timer, and get to the rear of the truck." He snatched the keys and flung them far out into the cotton field. Then he trained the 30-30 on the padlock that held the gate of the truck. The old timer's toothless mouth gaped open as he saw what was to come. The report of the rifle was muffled by the roar of the storm.

Bones had aimed well. He snatched the shredded padlock off and threw it into the mud. The old trusty's jaws worked noiselessly as he watched fifty hungry men boil out of the cattle truck. One mate grabbed at the rifle, Bones held; Bones backed off and levelled down on him.

"Give me the gun, Bones. I want to finish off that guard."

"Like hell you will." Bones worked the lever action jacking the extra loads out onto the ground. Then he jammed the barrel again and again into the mud until the whole barrel was chock full. Most of the mates were already slipping off towards the river. Bones yelled, "Don't stay in the river tonight! They'll have motorboats out!" Then, "Here's you a gun. Shoot it and you'll blow your head off." He pitched it on the ground, then wheeled and trotted off towards the heavy timber to the north. A few trotted after him a ways, then realizing they couldn't match his pace, turned and plunged down the banks toward the river.

The sullen faced mate stooped and picked up the

rifle and the muddy cartridges. He was the kind who only felt strong with a gun in hand. Today he had no time to clean the mudded barrel, but tomorrow . . .

It was already dark when the riderless horse returned to the prison. "Is that the Major's horse?"

"Hell no! That's not the Major's horse. Sound that alarm! Christ almighty!"

The cussing rasped like a chainsaw among the posse that rode out into the cotton fields, the chest-high cotton stalks crushing beneath the horses' thrust of hooves and legs churning in the wet sand. All the talk was of blood and killing. "Did Tyce get the hounds?"

"Hell, they can't trail in this rain. They won't be no good till mornin'. What we need's a damned alligator!"

The old trustee and two youngsters were still waiting by the truck when the posse rode up. The fury of the riders could be felt in the dark. The old trustee, out of experience, dropped his head between his knees so the blows would catch on his back. The two youngsters caught the clubs full in the teeth and nose. One guard yelled, "Hey, here's Burt!"

Four miles to the north, Bones gracelegged through the woods with the steady lope of a lean and hungry wolf.

## Chapter XXV, Texas Live Oak

*"If a bone eat a bone up a dry bone tree . . .*
*Guess this riddle and you can hang me."*

The first brief flush of joy at escape had vanished; now, nothing but slow steady jogging north into thicker woods until he felt safe to swing west towards the river. The night was absolute. Nighthawks and crickets alike slept. Bones hoped that damn prison was still asleep, but doubted it, his mind's eye picturing Cooney with the bloodhounds, the flashlights and rifles, the guards stirring out of their new brick homes. One guard, he knew for sure, slept and would not wake for a while.

The underbrush thicker now; he had counted four creeks he'd crossed in an hour's run, ticking off the names remembered from the maps. For the space of a quarter hour he had not heard any of his cellmates behind him. Bones, he thought, and the quirkiness of his name stuck in his mind. "They would need some of my bones to keep up." The pride of his Indian blood welled within him. All his life, he had run; all the runs of his life were now poured into this one run. As a boy he had run down jackrabbits till the jacks flopped over on their sides exhausted. When he was sixteen, he had run and walked a wild horse all day until the black mare stood stock still in her sweat, her sides heaving, and watched him walk up and slip the rope around her neck. He had not moved her then, but tied her to a small oak tree and went to sleep in the forks of the oak where any attempt to jerk free would wake him.

He would run two more hours and then hole up and sleep. That would put him 30 miles north and across Cypress Creek. Wade a half mile up Cypress and lose the dogs. The next night hit due west for the Brazos. The words kept forming on his lips, "Sleep in a tree, not on the ground. Sleep in a tree. Sleep in a tree."

Then a break from the woods, and fields which made the running easier. He thought he heard a dog bark, which caused his shoulders to drop by reflex, and his stride lengthen. Now, Highway 90, a thin ribbon of civilization, bound to be full of squad cars tomorrow. He knew this was the biggest break ever in Texas. Twenty years before in Arkansas, there was a bigger one. But Texas—always before, they slipped away only by twos and threes and singles.

Had an eye been watching the highway, it would scarcely have seen Bones slip across it on all fours, and would have mistook him for a coon or a possum. Here was a tank and a windmill. The cool water trickled down the side of his mouth, then on the back of his head where the rhythm of it drummed away some of his consciousness of fear.

After three solid hours of running, Bones knew he must be nearing Cypress Creek. Unless he had pointed too much at an angle toward the Northwest. Over his head the limbs of the huge Texas liveoaks stirred their leaves in a faint breeze. Then he began to plunge down an embankment he knew must be the big creek. In the water, thigh-deep, he stopped to drink again. The cows were asleep; their shit had long since settled, and he knew the water was clean. For ten, maybe fifteen minutes, he waded steadily upstream, not hiding his noise but not making much of it. Then he found his exit. A great oak sprawled by the creek bank, one of its limbs drooping near the water.

Bones hauled himself up out of the creek and into the tree. Sliding through to a limb extending out the other side he dropped to the ground forty feet from the creek. He jogged another two miles northwest before he stopped, desirous of a good headstart in case he heard the hounds pick up his trail tomorrow. He estimated he was at least ten miles further out than anyone else, and knew and counted upon the propensity of law men to flock wherever the first captures were being made. He also knew law men's minds walked in a straight line; they would start trailing from the prison, fanning out with hounds and guns, more than they would need, and never think to throw a circle of forty miles radius to cordon off the area, then draw it closed like a net. Bones had yet to see the law man whose mind could circle.

As luck would have it, he had entered a rocky patch of outcropping limestone. His prison issue brogans were dry now, and the leather landing on the rocks left no mark and but faint smell. Then he saw the tree.

Standing all alone, it was the grandaddy of live oaks. In the dim shadows of the night it spread and tumbled upwards towards the heavens, fold on fold, like a hindu temple. Approaching it gently on the hard sun-baked earth, Bones reached the outer limbs that swept the ground and began to climb. Hand over hand, from limb to limb, he squirreled his way up into the top of the white oak tree. Here a thick limb lay almost flat, and forked in two, but the one branch had twisted back and ran parallel to its brother.

His prison whites were caked with mud. His dark complected features were tanned to the color of pecan stain by the sun. Bones looked like nothing but the Indian he was. Stretching out on the limbs of the liveoak, with his shoulder in the trough, he felt the rough bark of the oak press against his cheek, and it reminded him of home. Not of one particular place or house he had lived at, nor of his parents, or wife and kin, *but simply of the word—of the thing of home.*

Desperate for sleep, he rubbed his tired thighs and shins through his pants. Now that he was still, he grew aware of his hunger. His mouth was wet, but his belly was almost empty. The guard he had knocked unconscious, and the thirty-five mile run had drained his strength from him. He knew he should eat something, even the oak leaves, so he could be ready for the morrow. Stirring, he felt something loose beneath his feet. He reached down and found the dry bones of some small animal. A squirrel perhaps, or a rabbit some hawk had picked clean on this perch sixty feet from the earth-floor.

Bones mused but a short while before he began to gnaw on the bones he had found up a dry bone tree. Dry at first until his teeth had crushed them and his saliva flowed into the bone meal, they began to taste in his mouth with the tang of meat and blood. By the time he had finished the handful of bones, his stomach had ceased to growl, his soul was dry, and the smack of his lips was as that of a king on his feast day. He stretched his limbs again upon the twin oak limbs and fell into a deep sleep. He dreamed, if dream it was, only of bones.

## Chapter XXVI BRAZOS DE DIOS

*"And in those banks to sleep and dream,*
*and in the river swim."*

Bones awoke to the sound of leaves scratching beneath the great live oak and then receding. Then a voice: "Nothing up that big tree as far as I can tell. Let's go on down to the creek. Sounds like the hounds might have picked up something. Probably no more than a ringtail."

Bones didn't know the voice. It must be some local law. If the dragnet's this far north, it means a lot of convicts are still loose. He looked for the scraps of the animal bones he had gnawed on last night. Likely they had saved his life; a bit of food in his belly was what let him sleep way up into the day—that and the deep foliage of the evergreen live oak that cut the sun. Well, best to simply stay up this tree till dark, and then make it to the river.

He found one slender bone he hadn't chewed on and put it in his pocket for a keepsake. Then he went back to sleep. A redbird fluttered down to a branch near his feet and looked curiously at him for a long time before it started singing. His sleep was sweetened by the redbird's song; his dream was the first sexual dream he had

had in a long time. In the dream a man and woman, naked, were curving around the trunk of a great tree with red bark. At first they were just touching, then they merged into each other, and as they merged they were changed into brightly-colored birds, perhaps woodpeckers, and the birds merged together. The dream kept returning to his light sleep; each time the glimpse of the naked man and woman was briefer until at last there seemed to be only bird.

When he woke again, the sun was going down and he had a hard bone in his britches. He started climbing down the tree.

Was it the earth unsteady or his legs? Quite a jog last night. Twenty-six, twenty-eight miles maybe. A marathon. The distance from Marathon to Athens.

He started jogging west towards the dying sun, towards the great river the Spanish called the Brazos de Dios, the Arms of God. The Brazos quicksandy, the Clear Fork, the Salt Fork, the Double Mountain Fork. The Brazos actually started in gullies in New Mexico a hundred miles west of Lubbock on the Llano Estacado. The salt fork that ran down off the Alkali flats gave the Brazos water its distinctive taste, to drink it left one thirstier than before. Bones had drank the water many times when he worked the ranch at Double Mountain. Old cowhands there, who recalled stories from older hands—long since dead and gone—would tell him that on the long trail herds up to Kansas after the War Between the States, the chuck wagon widow would take along an extra keg of salt to lace into the coffee so the cowpokes all the way across Oklahoma and Kansas could drink a bitter brew that tasted like coffee made with salty Brazos River water.

The Comanche, the old ones, had called the river Deep Blue Sky Water, Bones thought also, because of the salt, which—when the river narrowed and cleared in the summer—gave the deep holes of water a clear bluish cast; the river became a ribbon of Blue Holes.

The Brazos meant much to him, and all this flooded through his mind as he jogged along, keeping to the woods that lined the creek. Soon he would be in the river.

He smelled the smoke first, then caught the outlines of the wooden shack in the clearing. He walked quietly to a tree at the edge of the clearing and watched the house. He saw the denuded tree in the back with blue bottles stuck on the stubs of the limbs.

Niggers! Maybe he could scrounge some food!

There didn't seem to be a lot of people in the house. No car in sight. He heard only one set of feet occasionally scraping the wood floor of the shack. Then she came out on the porch and Bones saw her and knew the husband would not be far off. She was a tall buxom black woman with a glossy sheen on her round Ibo face and her neck and bare arms. She aimed the dishwater at a couple of Bantam chickens in the yard, then set the bucket on the porch and went back inside.

The house was built on the old style with mere piles of rocks serving as a foundation, the split pine shingles ending abruptly in the air on a line between the piles of rocks. Skunks took to houses like these like housecats to den up under.

Bones slid around among the trees to the side of the house where he could see through the kitchen window. She was stirring a pot of beans on the stove and humming the be-bop tunes the radio was playing. Her heavy breasts pushing against perhaps one petticoat and the thin cotton dress aroused him, but he knew this was not the time nor the place. Her man would be home soon. He needed the food though for his long swim south.

He had almost worked up his nerve to walk right up

and ask her for a bowl of beans when his chance came. She sat the pot of beans in the window to cool, then, unbuttoning her dress as she went, turned towards the back room of the house, evidently to change clothes. In a flash Bones' eyes—which had followed the unfolding black womanflesh out of sight—went back to the beans; in a flash, he had grabbed the hot iron handle and carried the beans behind the big burr oak tree.

He sat the hot iron pot down and dug into the dark wet loam to cool his hand. Then, the action almost outrunning the thought, he scooped a couple of handfuls of the cool loam into the pot to cool the beans. She had sliced some cayenne, ginger, and tomatoes into the beans, Cajun style, and Bones wolfed it down with relish. When he had eaten his fill, the pot was empty. He pitched it back over beneath the window sill where it hit a rock giving out a sharp iron ring. He ducked deeper into the bush and waited.

She came out still fastening a red calico dress that was cut wide and low in front. She stooped slowly and picked up the pot and walked deliberately up on the porch, then spoke in a voice too loud to be talking to herself, "Reckon a coon's done got my beans. Henry will have to settle for cornbread and honey tonight." Then she entered, closed and latched the door, set down the pot, and leaned her back against the door, hugging her breasts with her arms. Her breath came short and hard.

Bones was already running through the woods.

Then he was in the river. Swollen from the rains and heated by the day's worth of burning sun, the water closed about him like the juice in his mother's womb. Half-bank full, and luckily, here he entered from the deep side. He soon found the current and began to swim with it, silent as the catfish beneath him. Using a breast stroke, only his shock of black hair and nose stuck out of the water; though the night was clear he seemed no more than a turtle on the skin of the river.

When he tired of the breast stroke, he would roll over on his back and swim like a frog kicking his arms and legs in a flat plane beneath the surface of the river. One powerful stroke and he could coast for thirty feet, his body buoyed by the kick and the deep breath he took between strokes.

In the night sky he could see Orion's broad belt. The hunter of the night sky; how often he had guided William Bones back to his door after a long night's hunt with the hounds. And there was Aldebaran. Was Orion stalking the bull, or had he already slain Taurus and now sought the daughters, the lovely Pleiades. Whatever, there came the Scorpion not far behind ready to sting the heel again.

A fish broke water near his head. *Yellowcat* he mused. Or *Appaloosa,* that strange hybrid between Yellow and Blue cat the fellow from the Game and Fish department had swore up and down didn't exist. He could grabble fish tomorrow. He would not go hungry.

There was patience as well as urgency in his swim. Time was on his side now. He knew the wont of man to hunt only what could be easily found. With each hour, his trail grew colder. The rain had washed most of it into the river. Had he killed the guard with the rifle butt? Hopefully not. Can't look back. Blind instinct called that shot. Reason stuffed the mud in the gun barrel. Curiously enough, it was the beetle blind lightning that turned the wheel. It would be hell for the ones left on the farm for a couple of weeks, and worse hell for those that are caught, but less hell with the Major gone. His brand of sadism was rare, even among guards.

Three days and nights he was in the Brazos. By night he swam, a strange fish among the carp and buffalo, the catfish and turtles. By day he would crawl up into a clump of willows and pull the alder about him until he was hid even from the bluejays. When the first light drove the channelcats into the shade of the rocks on the deep side of the channel, he would grabble. Running his hand along their unfeeling bellies until he could lock thumb, forefinger and middle behind the gill fins, sharp as knives, and snatch the catfish out of the water. Then, carefully avoiding the long needles of the dorsal fins that flexed on the back, he would snap the heads off the catfish, and rip out their entrails with his hand. Using his teeth as pliers, he would peel the tough skin back and eat the tender, boneless flesh of the fish. Twice he was finned on his hands, but the salty Brazos water quickly healed his wounds. Once he caught a gar that brushed his leg. Acting out of habits he learned from his father, he broke the spear of the gar's snout and gave it back to the river to die.

Near the aptly named town of Freeport, on the third night, the old *Brazos de Dios* emptied Bones into the Gulf of Mexico. The hard packed sand at low tide made for good running; he had long since thrown away his prison shoes. Now his legs stretched out to the northeast along the spit of land that ran out toward the island called Galveston.

## Chapter XXVII OLD GALVESTON

Still hiding by day in the dunes and scrub oak, and running the coast by night, Bones reached the city limits of Galveston the following morning just as the rose fingered dawn was peeling back the curtain of the sky. A few kitchen lights were on where men were preparing to go to work in the refineries in Bay City and their women were fixing their lunches or they were fixing their own.

Bones spotted an old car, a '48 Dodge, which he knew was easy to hotwire. The door was unlocked. He slid behind the wheel and quietly pulled the door to the first catch, then bent over the ignition attached to the steering column. The wires pulled loose easily. He stripped the coating off with his teeth, made hooks in the ends and carefully hooked them together as his foot depressed the clutch. The motor turned and caught. *Tuned up! It purrs like a kitten.*

The Dodge quietly rolled away, Bones slowly raising his head above the wheel to see where he was going. He had been in Galveston once to visit an old cousin of his father's who still taught *Redwing* on the piano and guitar to young kids after school. He decided to drive by her house. Sure enough, there was the huge camphor tree and the swing on the front porch. He fancied he could hear her well-tuned piano playing in the morning dark.

Then he was out onto the causeway leaving Galveston behind. Houston lay ahead.

On the side roads he didn't glance at the gas gauge until he had entered the little town of Dickinson, named for the captain at the Alamo whose widow, alone with a baby and a slave, were left to tell the tale. The gauge showed empty. He coasted his short down a dark shady side street and killed the motor. Had to get a change of clothes before it got light. As muddy as these prison whites were, they didn't look like the standard fare.

He climbed a fence and started walking through back yards. The third one was luck. Some men's work clothes covered the clothesline. He grabbed a pair of Dickies' pants and a khaki shirt that looked about right and climbed two more yards until he paused to change clothes. Even with the cover of a cedar tree, Bones was worried. It was starting to get light. Soon a multitude on the streets. Hunger gnawed inside. He could see faintly through the rear window of the house. Was that an icebox?

He bundled up his clothes and moved cautiously towards the rear of the house. Just as he reached the window, a light snapped on in the kitchen and a woman in the house was looking directly at him. She showed no surprise and was so calm Bones believed she hadn't seen him. She pulled her robe tight and bustled about the kitchen. Bones could not quite see what she was reaching for in a drawer.

Then he saw. She had an old Smith and Wesson .38 and was calmly placing a bullet in the chamber. She turned and pointed the blue steel revolver at the window where she had seen the hawklike face, but Bones was done gone *like a turkey through the corn, with his longjohns on.*

A young girl in her nightgown came into the kitchen. "Mama, whatcha doin' with that pistol."

"There was a man at the window."

"A man! At this hour?"

"Yep! One of those convicts that 'scaped from Sugarland I reckon. I just pointed this at him and scared him off."

"Oh, Mom. You're too much. You make it sound just like out of a novel! You gonna call the law?"

"Nope. He's gone and won't be back. I heard him go over the fence. There's no need to call the law into it."

Bones was gone. He hotfooted it back to the short-wired Dodge, which he started up again. However much gas there was in the car, it would get him further faster than he could go on foot. So he took the Dodge out of Dickinson the way he had come and drove back across the causeway into Old Galveston. He figured if the woman had called the law, they would look for him to head to Houston first.

Galveston, where Jean Lafitte held forth for a long time, and even when the U.S. Navy sent a fleet after him, saw it coming in time to burn his place to the ground and set sail for the far reaches of the Caribbean. Galveston, it was here that LaSalle first saw the Osage Orange with its huge pigapples and gave it the enticing name of Bois D'Arc.

Galveston, can't stay long. I'm Louisiana bound.

Bones parked the Dodge just off U.S. 87 near the north end of the island, and decided to take a chance hitchhiking along the coast. The fifth one along, an old retired farmer in a black, beat-up Ford pickup, stopped and said, "Hop in."

"You going to Louisiana?"

"Lake Charles. Does that suit you?"

"That'll be a big help. I'm much obliged for the lift."

"Think nothin' of it."

So he left old Galveston, and soon would leave old Texas. As he watched the bayous and swamps and flat coastal plain pass by, he felt like Sugarland was becoming part of an ancient past he would recall only in his dreams.

The farmer said little, just chewed tobacco and spit out the window, and listened to a little country music on the radio. "Here, have a chew of this tobakker. It's Bloodhound."

"Thanks. I will."

"You'll have to spit in this paper sack, though. My missus don't like tobacco stains on that side of the truck where she gets in."

"Certainly."

As they neared Port Arthur, the old farmer reached under the seat and pulled out a shapeless broad-brimmed black felt hat that had seen better days. "Here, try one of my hats on. It'll keep your ears warm."

A flash of Bones' eyes showed his gratitude. He knew his prison haircut had given him away, and he knew this old man knew something about life to act as he did.

Soon, Lake Charles, then Opelousas, and New Orleans. There, he knew he would meet up again with Connors.

As they neared the high bridge over the Sabine, the farmer switched his radio set to a New Orleans station. "Better music," was all he said.

The first song they heard was one by Bob Wills and the Texas Playboys, called "Remember My Faded Love." Bones looked down at the lovely Sabine, yellow and muddy. The plaintive fiddle stirred an old memory of the woman he had fought over and for whom he had killed the man, which sent him to Sugarland. Her lips had been that sweet. He'd fight for her again, though now he knew she wasn't worth the trouble. Now the fiddles were in full voice and it was as if the bows were sawing on the insides of his ribs. Unknown to himself, he was humming.

His heart grew light as a feather within his chest as they passed into Louisiana. For a while, even the memory of Sugarland faded from sight. His eyes blurred from a bit of moisture, then closed. His head rolled back against the seat and he went to sleep. A slim smile flitted across the face and tobacco lips of the old farmer.

## Chapter XXVIII: A LETTER FROM BARATARIA

Daryl Barnes
Danville, Texas

Daryl,

Thought I would write to let you know they haven't caught me yet. I can't stay in one place any too long, so can't expect to hear back from you. But, I'll know if and when you get this letter from me.

You asked me once what made Sugarland the way it was, and if all prisons were the same way. The first part of that is hard to answer, though I'll try. The answer to the second part is yes. Any prison takes away what men have always held most dear next to life itself, their freedom. In all the time men have been here, they've only had the two ways of controlling those who didn't fit in, killing them and jailing them. And they couldn't keep many in jail for long without the fear of death hanging over their heads.

Texas prisons, and I aint been to no others though I've talked to those who have, might have a refinement on the system. It's not that they work a man to death, though I saw that happen. It's that they break a man's spirit through backbreaking work.

After a few years, or with some a few months, a man aint fit for no kind of life but prison life. That's why they told you at Sugarland that once you were in the system you couldn't get out, that the average time parolees were on the outside was only nine months before they were back inside the walls.

If I know you Daryl, you will make your parole. It will be hard. Every time something happens, someone will point the finger at you. The law will try to hum you back into jail for nothing. The reason is because you know something they don't. You know the limits of what any man, any law, can do to you. You know what it is to be a slave, which means you know what it is to be free. You know especially what it is to be an outlaw, and for this society can never forgive you. They can not bear to understand all your actions. Their fear leads them to believe you are ready to break their laws at any moment. This is because they secretly hold their laws in contempt, knowing that law in and by itself neither can comprehend nor control all the passions of men. Only songs and poetry encompass it all. Most law is written by men who don't have much song and poetry in them.

Just a few more words, and I still don't know if I've answered your question as to what made Sugarland the way it was. One thought comes to mind. It wasn't always that way, and when change comes, it's not always for the worse. When you make your parole, it might be wise for you to clear out of the state for awhile, so you can shake the fear of the law that will still be in the back of your head. Take off up to Wyoming or Montana, or maybe even Alaska, into the back country where they don't ask much of a man, but can he work. Ha! Daryl, can you work? Boy, can you work!

Here's a twenty I found by the wayside. I hope it

comes in handy. Don't worry none about me. There's nothing here but ticks, chiggers, fleas, and gators, gars, and coons. And now and then the wind whistling through the liveoaks.

your friend,
William Bone

P.S. Never fail to remember.
Justice lies in men, not in laws.

Daryl folded the letter back up and stuffed it in his shirt pocket and buttoned it up. He knew he would need to draw on it again. A new Chevrolet pickup was pulling into Harris' Humble station, and that meant work. One of the Deever brothers.

"Howdy. Fill it up with regular. And there's a flat tire in the back that needs patching. I'm walking over yonder to get me a Dairy Cream and I want it fixed by the time I get back."

"It'll get fixed when it gets fixed."

"Boy, are you talking back to me?"

"No. And I'm not your boy. You can only fix a flat so fast, and I'll get to it as soon as I pump your gas." Daryl went ahead with cleaning the windshield, not bothering to look at Deever.

Deever muttered, "That's better," and sauntered over to the Dairy Cream to throw some of his forty-five year-old small talk at the cute little fourteen year-old waitress who served up the whipped milk and sno-cones.

Daryl hefted the truck tire out of the back end, and set about breaking it down. The tire was worn, and it wouldn't matter much about patching the tube; it would keep going flat. Daryl found the big mesquite thorn. Sure enough, Deever had gone chasing some cows in some rough country. Too damn lazy to get a horse, or to cut his mesquites. Thinks he can just run right over them. Serves him right. Hell, I shouldn't say that.

The tire patched and aired up, Daryl pitched the tire iron back down on the concrete, listening to the sharp ring of the steel. He had already slung the tire back in the pickup when Deever returned.

"That will be $4.50, $3.50 for the gas and a dollar for the flat."

Deever counted out ones from his wallet, and then grudgingly counted out nickels and dimes from his watch pocket. Finally there was enough, and he handed it to Daryl, a slight smirk on his face. Then, pitching into the cab, he drove off.

Grady Harris was back from lunch now, and Daryl appreciated the company, even though business was slow. Grady might not say much, but he was good people; Daryl knew not many in town would have given him a chance. About one-thirty, a whole batch of cars and trucks swung into the service station. Daryl jumped up from the back of the garage, and made for the door, thankful at least there was some work. His heart sunk when he saw who it was: Deever, the sheriff, and the stump-armed constable. Grady was just as quick boiling out of the office.

"What's the matter, Sheriff?"

"Harris, Roy Deever here says that Barnes stole a truck tire from him, a tire he was supposed to fix, and that he had the gall to charge him anyway for fixing the flat."

"That's a lie!"

"Now, hold on there, Daryl. Let me hear this out."

"Deever says that by the time he got to town and looked back in the bed and saw the tire wasn't there, he came and got me. He's ready to swear out a complaint, and if he does, I'll have to take Barnes in."

Grady squinted into the sun, spat out a stream of tobacco juice from the big plug of Day's Work he kept in his jaw, and said, "Well, Sheriff, let's hear the other side of the story before we jump to any conclusions. Daryl, how about it?"

"It's a lie. I fixed that flat on that old worthless tire and put it back into the truck. Deever knows damn well I did."

"That's Mr. Deever to you, Barnes. If you can't say more than that, I'll have to take you in, and you know what that means, being on parole."

"There's no way I could have stole it. I haven't been anywhere but this filling station. Now, if you can find that tire here, go ahead, and I'll go with you."

"He's right, Sheriff. I've been back from lunch a half hour now, and Barnes hasn't been anywhere, and we haven't had a customer. If he stole that tire, then it's still here. If it's here, you can have him.

Blake saw he had been caught, and said, "Sam, take a look around for a Chevy tire mounted on a wheel that will match Deever's truck."

Deever broke in for the first time, his beefy face redder than usual. "That don't mean anything. He has had plenty of time to hide it."

After a moment or so, Sam reported back. "There's nothing like that around here."

Blake wasn't used to being made a fool of, and there was something else at stake here, his authority. "Well, I believe I'm going to have to take you down, anyway, Barnes, for questioning, at least until we come up with that tire."

Grady Harris had served four years with the seabees in the Pacific during the war, and he knew something of how to measure men, and what they are capable of. He spoke quickly and firmly. "Sheriff, if you take Barnes in, you'll have to take me. I know he didn't steal any tire, and you know it. If you take him, you're calling me a liar. I've never been to jail, and I think I don't even know how to go."

There was menace in the last words, and Blake knew it. If he'd been ten years younger, he wouldn't have taken that off any man. But Harris was burly with thick arms honed by heavy work. Blake didn't need to mess with him. Better to bite back down the road he'd come up. "Hellfire, Deever, if you didn't see him take it, and it's not around here, what in the world makes you so damn sure he took it."

Deever was scared of the sheriff, himself, now. "I . . . I don't know. Maybe somebody else after I got downtown and parked by the feedstore."

Barnes was a bit reckless now, sensing they had won the battle of words. "Not a soul in town would have stole that worthless tire from you."

Blake reddened. "Shut up, Barnes. You don't know how close you came to getting run in today."

Then they were gone, the big Hudson swaying back out onto the highway followed by the constable's Plymouth and Deever's Chevrolet pickup. Harris spoke first, "If they had busted you, what would have happened? Would they have sent you back down to the farm?"

"Yeah, they sure would have."

"That's what I thought. Well, you were lucky. A smarter fool than Deever would have framed you better. Keep your nose cleaner than Ben Jensen's funeral parlor, and next time, if you wait on people while I am gone to lunch, let me know. Better yet, I think I'll start brownbagging my lunch. If that damn sheriff wants you back in the pen that bad, it may be I better stick around here all the time." He turned then to go back to work.

Daryl blurted out a quick "Thanks!"

Harris smiled a bit, as if to himself, "Don't mention it. Hell, I enjoyed it!"

## EPILOGUE: NEW ORLEANS

*Hush that crying, honey dear,*
*Jackson Square remains still here*
*In sunny New Orleans*
*In lovely Louisiana.*

Bones had spent two weeks camped out on the small bayou in Jefferson Parish south of Barataria. Each day his jaunts carried him a bit farther afield. Perhaps tomorrow he would go on into New Orleans. Give the post offices a little time to cover his mug with a few other wanteds. Barataria and Lafitte were such small sleepy towns and post offices that the half dozen wanted signs in each were about ten years old. New Orleans, he knew, would be different; there every wanted poster that came in the mail would be plastered up. Regulations.

Figuring to get a head start the next day he decided to sleep in the front seat of an old abandoned truck near the railroad tracks that ran off south to Grand Isle. The upholstery had long since gone, eaten by moths or carried away by birds, but plenty of horsehair still covered the springs, so Bones actually thought it would be fine sleeping compared to his bed of leaves down on the creek. So he made his supper out of a bit of jerky and some crackers he had got that morning at the little country store, then curled up and went to sleep, not even bothering to take off his stolen brogan shoes, as he did on the creek. The slingshot he had made to kill squirrels with and his few other belongings were folded up in his black hat and made for a pillow.

In the morning, the sun was up, but it wasn't the sun that awakened him. It was something like a bird cry. There it was again. Not a bird. Something almost like it; then he heard the footsteps. One step up on the running board of the cab. Through half-lidded eyes, he saw two eyes, white in a round black face, peer up and over to where he lay, then widen like saucers—"HOBO SHOES!"

And he leapt down off the cab. Bones sat up just in time to see the two eight year-olds dusting leather down the tracks. "Ha! Ha! *Hobo shoes.* I reckon so."

"Well, better get going if I'm gonna make Orleans today." Outside the cab he stretched, put his things in his pockets, shaped the black hat the best he could and placed it on his head. He didn't need it so much now since the hair on the back of his neck and his sideburns had grown out. But he liked it, and it made him fit the landscape better than he had supposed possible. There were a lot of shapeless broad-brimmed black hats in these parts.

He walked to Barataria and about a half mile out of town stuck his thumb out. The third one along gave him a lift. "Howdy."

"Where you headed?"

"To Town."

"I'm going to Canal Street."

"That's fine. What's your load?"

"Some cordwood for the barbecue joints."

"Post Oak?"

"Nope. Live Oak."

"Seasoned?"

"Yep."

And so, back and forth the laconic talk, and then they were up high over the father of waters, on a bridge built, according to the sign, by Huey Long—who built a lot of bridges, singlehandedly—settling down into New Orleans.

When he stopped to let Bones off on Canal Street, the woodsman shot out his slender black hand, "Good luck to you."

Bones felt the calluses on his palm and knew he had cut a lot of hardwood in his time, and that not all with a crosscut saw. "Much obliged to you. What do I owe you?"

"Not a dime," and the grin widened into a broad smile. "So long."

"So long."

Bones walked west from Canal Street and towards the river until he knew he was in the heart of where poor people lived. He spotted an old dark woman with silver hair pinched in a bun hanging out clothes. "Afternoon."

"Good afternoon to you. Whatcha sellin'?"

"Aint sellin' nothing."

"Then whatcha want?"

"I need just a place to sleep. I'm broke and looking for work. I'll be glad to do some chores, chop wood, anything, for a place to bed down."

"Will a chicken house do?"

"Are there lots of chickens in it?"

"Just two little banties, but they won't bother you."

"Yes ma'am. That will do fine."

She led him inside to her kitchen and fixed him a lunch of warmed up rice and crawfish, then showed him some fresh hay to make his pallet in the chicken coop.

Hoping to get an early start in the morning, at sundown he stretched out in his hobo shoes on the straw pallet, lay his hat over his face in case one of the two speckled banties decided to roost overhead, and went to sleep. Civilized now with a roof over his head. Given the chicken smell, he liked the bayou better.

* * *

For a week he walked down to the docks every morning, finding a little pickup work offloading bananas and vegetables, and asking about the ships headed south, if they needed any hands. In the afternoons he would have a cup of coffee at Jackson Square and watch the world go by, then later catch the St. Charles streetcar to the end of the line and back. There was something about the peacefulness of the large live oaks that stretched their leafy limbs nearly across St. Charles that appealed to him. Compared to the short prison barbered oaks at Sugarland, these exuded age, respect and repose.

On Sunday, the docks were quiet. Bones decided to take a walk around to see if he could stir up his old friend. No cops were in sight; if any were on duty, he knew they, too, would be infected by the lazy atmosphere of the warm Sunday morning and linger long over their chicory-laced coffee in the Quarter.

By a natural inclination he was drawn to a section of old New Orleans that was rundown, but not too rundown. The big two-story Victorian houses were still solid if unpainted. A lot of liquor stores and bars. Only blacks on the streets, old grandmothers, parasols warding off the sun, leading their families to church, and old winos who probably slept off their Saturday night fling on these same streets, and who now blinked their eyes like a lazy bass at the sun that forbade their sleep.

Twice Bones had walked by a large old Victorian that looked to be in particular good trim. A fancy light on the doorstep made him think whoever lived there might do some fair entertaining now and then. Each time he sauntered past, he had thought he'd seen the curtain move in a second story window as if someone was always watching out.

This time he just stood across the street, looking casually up and down the sidewalk. Then it struck him. He took off his broad-brimmed black hat that shaded his eyes and ran his hand through his shock of black hair. The curtain moved.

Scarcely a moment passed before a twelve year-old boy who looked old and wise about the eyes came running out of the house and accosted Bones on the street. "Follow me. My boss wanta talk to you."

"How do I know I want to talk to him?"

"He says to ax you if you remember old Midnight."

Bones kept a straight stern face on for the boy. "Well, let's see this boss of yours. Let's see if he's got more to say for himself than you do. Coming out here talking in riddles. Hmhh! Old Midnight! Hmhh!"

"Boss aint gonna like it if you's mad."

Bones didn't answer but followed the boy up the steps, through the wide door and up the stairs to a landing that opened into many rooms. On the landing, a broad smile splitting his face and a few happy tears blurring his eyes, stood Connors.

"Let me LOOK at you, man!" They hugged each others like brothers who hadn't seen each other in years, or like bears about to fight over a blackberry patch. The boy, embarassed by the affection, ambled off down the hall, lifting a deck of cards from his hip pocket.

Connors led him into an elegantly laid-out parlor and deftly poured some whiskey in three tall glasses. "Benna! Benna! Come look who's paying us a visit. You don't have to dress up. It's kinfolks!"

"Bones! Bones, where you been, man. I been readin' about you in the papers. Where you stayin'?"

"I'm sleeping a few blocks north of here in a chicken coop."

"Ha! Ha! Did you hear that, Benna? Bones is holed up in a real hen house!" Benna strolled into the room wearing only a black slip cut low over her full breasts, cut high up on her thighs, and with a red bandana wrapped around her hair. She picked up her whiskey and curled up in Connors' lap.

"Is this the man you told me about, honey?"

"Yep, that's him."

"Why, he don't look like an escaped convict. He look like a preacher maybe, or a railroad conductor."

"Sugar, do *I* look like an escaped *convict?"*

They all burst out laughing as Connors gestured at his pressed blue-silk shirt and black tapered trousers of highly polished cotton.

"Yep. That's him. Billy Bones. When he escaped, he took a truck full with him. Fifty souls fled the gates of Sugarland that day."

Bones poured himself some more whiskey and asked, "How many of them are still loose?"

"Seven. Seven out of fifty. You, Givens, and five more are still on the loose."

"Flores?"

"Yep. Flores is still loose. Probably plumb to Monterey by now. But you, Bones! You're as loose as a goose. Look at him, Benna! Don't he look like an alligator man?"

"He looks like all he gotta do is smile and them crawdads would crawl right up into his lap."

Connors' laughter hit the rafters. Bones almost smiled in spite of himself.

"Tell me Conroy . . . were any of them killed?"

"Yep," Connors spoke soberly, "Two of them were shot when captured, supposedly because they tried to escape. One was real peculiar, though. The White boy was shot in an abandoned farmhouse, and guard that shot him then put his ought-six in his mouth and blowed his own head off. He died of *self-inflicted* gunshot wounds, as the papers put it."

"That's usually the case. Whenever there's an escape, if any guards get it, they'll kill a convict on capture for every guard that got aced."

"But only one guard died. . . ."

"What! Was that the Major?"

"Yep, and they didn't say what killed him; you talk about funny . . ."

"Funny!" Bones laughed, a short bark-like laugh. "Connors, that was a sight if there ever was one. I see I'll have to tell you my getaway first, but at least that young guard didn't die, but never mind that. This is the way it went down."

Benna and Connors both shifted their heads slightly apart to hear Bones better, she scarcely conscious of her near nakedness, the brown flesh accented sharply by the bare black slip and the red bandana atop her head like a brakeman's flag.

"Let me have some more whiskey first, 'cause it's dry in the telling." He poured Connors another draught, also. "We were pickin' cotton, laying down them long rows, that long cotton sack draggin' like a ball and chain. A huge thunderstorm boiled up out of the Gulf. I tell you, Connors, all of a sudden I looked up and there was the ocean up in the sky, all blue and black. I was ready to make for the barn, but you know that skunkass Major; he hated the elements for making him do something different, and he was gonna make us pick till the lightning struck. And, boy, we could see it a'coming. You talk about chain lightning! Each stalk of that lightning followed the other so fast, you never saw it disappear. That lightning came like dozens of yellow snakes yanking on the sky. Walking lightning, I call it.

"Well, finally, even the Major got scared enough to quit, and we headed for the wagon. I was draggin' my sack cause I thought when that rain hit, they wouldn't see me slipping off. Now, you're not gonna believe any of this and I don't care if you do or not. But I'm telling it to you. I was might near the wagon and I heard Givens call it down on him. These are his exact words. Givens said, *'I wish to God lightning would strike him dead,'* and sure enough a blue ball of fire hit that demon Major right where his ass turns into lard."

Connors and Benna both burst out laughing, their eyes still slightly incredulous at the tale.

"Well, it knocked him for a loop, and two of the other three guards carried him off between them. I saw my chance and jumped in the cotton. Two of the boys, one was Flores, covered me with their sacks. The storm had hit full blast. The rain was like sleet, it was coming so thick and fast.

"So just as the truck pulled the wagon out onto the river road, I made my play. I hopped out, swung that wagon into the ditch, and when the guard wheeled around on his mare, I followed her from behind and dog-eared her from the blind side. You oughta seen the look on that guy's face. Then I grabbed his rifle and hit him a good lick up aside the head, feared that I killed him. You sure relieved my mind on that point.

"Well, the old trustee had given up trying to pull that cotton trailer, two-thirds full, out of that ditch with the old Mack truck, and he just killed the motor and sat there. I shot the lock off the truck and all the boys boiled out of there like angry yellowjackets and hightailed it for the river. One of them nearly jumped me. He was itchin' to plug the guard, so I rammed the gunbarrel in the mud. Then I lit out North, and ran about twenty-five mile that first night. I knew there was some timber up that way and a lot of creeks to lose the dogs in.

"The next night I turtled down to the old quick-sandy Brazos and swum by night till I reached the Gulf. My closest call came in the little town of Dickinson where one of them militant housewives loaded up a .38 to plug me between the eyes. She would have, too. She was a cool one. I suspect many an escapee had crossed through that neck of the woods to disturb her equilibrium.

"So, the old timer who gave me a lift into lovely Louisiana gave me this hat to hide my shaved head. I hid out in the swamps a couple of weeks, and I done been in town a whole week askin' around about you. Ain't nobody in town seems to have ever heard of Conroy. You keep a mightly low profile."

"Ha! Ha! Have you ever heard the likes of that, Benna Mae?"

"Yeah! Just NOW!"

"Ha! Ha! Ha! Bones, you're sure somethin'. Listen, Benna. Why don't you pull a dress on over your head and run get your friend, Cora, and tell her to come hear this story." He ran his wide hand across the expanse of her breasts. "As much of you as there is, it still aint enough for me and Bones, too. I 'spect you're needing a woman bad, aren'tcha, Bones?"

If Bones' blush could have showed through his deep tan, it would have showed. "Well, y-yes. As a matter of fact. Yes! But, don't put yourself out none."

"Don't you worry, Billy. He ain't puttin' *himself* out. Can I call you *Billy?*"

"Certainly you can."

"Well, when you see Cora, you'll know this fool here just wants her over here to give her what he calls a good lookin' over."

"Ha! Git along gal. Bones here could have been drowned in the river or sucked into quicksand. We got a lot of celebratin' to do. Cora's off work tonight, so you won't have to buy her way out of the bar. Here's a couple of Andy Jacksons, no, you'll need another one. Stop by and get some ribs, some chicken and gumbo and some of that black label whiskey that comes out of Tennessee."

Benna had pulled on a bright yellow cotton dress patterned with small green and white daisies, that fit her snugly all around. She had a green silk parasol and a plumed blue hat to match. She lifted the three bills out of Connors' nonchalant hand and tucked them into her bosom, giving him a light kiss on his still outstretched fingers. She smiled wide and deep at Bones, indecipherable knowledge intuitive in her dark brown eyes. "I'll be back before too long!" and she flounced off.

Bones and Connors just sat still for a while pulling at their whiskeys. Now and then Connors would say, sort of to himself, "That's some story, alright. Some story."

Finally, Bones stirred. "Tell me about your breakout, Conroy. Have you still got that paint horse?"

"How! I wish I had. There aint too much to tell. I sneaked word out through Abercrombie to Benna and Truck—that's Truck's boy that brought you up—and they did the rest. I just rode that old Paint right through that fence—of course Truck had cut a hole for me—jumped the barditch and rode him right up into the trailer. Truck took off before I even had the tailgate up. We sold that old Paint in Monroe for two hundred dollars, and that was my stake in this here business I got now."

"What kind of business is it. Looks like you did mighty well starting off with just two bills."

"Well, we play a few cards, some gallopin' dominoes, you *know. . . .*"

"Sounds mighty good to me. By the way, what do they call you? Benna looked a little funny when I called you Conroy."

"She hadn't heard that one. She calls me Eldred, my given name. Sounds funny, huh?"

"Nope. It makes you sound wise."

"Wheeoo! Wise . . .? Wiseacre, mebbe."

"What about this here Cora?"

"Well, she's a red skin a bit like you. Wild as a March wind. If you can get ahold of her, she'll turn you every way but loose."

"Has she got a fellow?"

"Nope. She did have, but I kinda ran him off the other day. When I heard you'd escaped, I figured she'd be an ideal match to strike you some fire. He owed me a little money, so it weren't no trouble."

"Well, it's been so long since I talked to a woman, I might not think of much to say."

"Listen to me. When you see her, if you can still say '*howdy,*' you'll be doing fine."

"Aw, go on Connors. How you talk!"

* * *

"What's this man, Bones, like, Benna?"

"Why he aint like nothing you ever saw. He don't say too much. But when he starts talkin', well, let's just say that your stomach can get all churned up inside."

"Is that what happened to you?"

"Now, Cora, don't you go gettin' jealous when you haven't met the man. I'm happy with Eldred, but if I wasn't, I wouldn't let any grass grow under my feet 'fore I latched onto this here Billy Bones."

"Do you reckon he'll cotton to me?"

Benna scanned Cora's shape in her snug, sleeveless cotton dress. "If he dudn't, he'll deserve a switchin', for sure. And I'll give it to him."

"Surely. I just bet you will. . . ."

Cora was all and more than Connors had implied. Sure enough when he saw her, Bones couldn't think of a thing to say. Choctaw she was, mostly, some Ibo or Benin, some French, and something else—Portuguese maybe. Tall, about five-nine, in her sleeveless cotton dress and matching white pumps she walked about the room like a puma ready to spring. Round high-cheeked face, full at the breasts, but lithe and slim in waist, hips and legs, she drank whiskey like a man, and sure enough, *she* had plenty to say . . .

"So this is Billy Bones! And I thought I was going to meet the Second Coming! Why Eldred Connors, he looks just like a scarecrow in my mother's cornfield, and like a scarecrow, he just sits there and doesn't say hide nor hair."

Bones eyes watched her every move, and bore into the pith of her like two bright black suns. She saw he had the sign of The People, too, in his brow and nose.

"Cora Lee. What a pore mouth you picked up on the side of the road. Bones is my best friend. He not only helped to spring me. He saved my life while in prison."

"Oh yeah? How'd he do that?" Bones could tell she was just nervous because it was a set-up situation. He remembered how he had ran and walked that wild horse all day until he caught it. When he finally slipped a rope around its neck, it was gentle as a fawn. She, too, would gentle down when she stopped running.

"We was clearing timber with just axes. Mostly scrub-oak and sumac. We was talkin' a bit. All of a sudden out of the corner of my eye I saw Bones' axeblade coming at my leg. I jumped high up. His axe hit the ground. I was plumb shook up. This *bull* threw a shell into the chamber of his winchester and I thought my number was up. Then Bones reaches down and holds up this big diamondback rattler that he had done chopped the head off of. Boy, if that rattler had got ahold of my leg I'd of turned into poison."

Bones spoke, "You're already a pretty poison, Connors. Next time I'll let that grandaddy snake bite you and we'll see which poison wins out."

The brittleness broke inside Cora at the sound of his

west Texas twang, and her laugh went way down in her throat and chest. Benna and Connors laughed hard, too. Benna rubbed Connors' neck, "Let me have some of that poison, honey. You been holdin' out on me."

"Why, I'll swan," Cora purred, "why didn't you tell me he was just plain *folks?*"

"Cause that's all I ever was. Just plain *folks.* We were trying to keep you from finding that out."

And the laughter rippled again through the sunlit parlor, warm as the whiskey singing through the bloodstream.

"Besides, I been drinking straight whiskey for an hour with Connors, the first touch I've had in five years. It's a wonder I can even say *Howdy* to you."

"Well, *howdy* stranger."

"Howdy, yourself."

"Just fine. Might I call you *Billy?* I don't want to be behind my friend, Benna, here. She's a mighty strong attraction."

"You just might, if you'll wear that smile for a minute more, and if that don't wear it out."

Cora smiled so wide she clapped her hand over her mouth, but still couldn't hide her pleasure at this small talk. Her discomfort had shifted into such an acute liking for this dark taciturn stranger she was feeling shy again. Her way out was to do something she loved to do. "If y'all will move to the supper table, I'll have that gumbo hot before you know it. We got to get Billy some food; why he ain't nothing but a heap of *Bones!*"

"You would be too, eating that Sugarland special morning, noon, and night."

"Eldred says it was mighty rough."

"If I told you about it for a month of Sundays, then you would still only know the half of it."

"I'll be glad to listen."

"Well, today's Sunday. I reckon we can get started."

They sat around the table and ate the ribs, and chicken gumbo, and cornbread and butter, and drank whiskey on ice until it was dark and the car traffic on the street had died down. Cora, as she talked and listened, glowed golden in the soft yellow light and made Bones recall the beautiful *'yaller gal'* that Leadbelly used to sing about.

After supper Connors produced some Cuban cigars and some brandy. Benna said she had never seen him this mellow.

"Bones, what I been meaning to ask you, and just now got around to it, is this. Where you gonna go from here?—You can throw in with me if you like."

"Thanks Connors. I'll always be obliged to you for that offer. There's nothing I'd like better. I just might take you up on that in a few years. The heat's still on me though. I can feel it prickling the back of my neck. You know those Texas Rangers that aint got nothing to do, well, they're fanning out all over the South looking for my mug. I've made contact with this banana boat heading to Guatemala in a week. They'll let me work my way to Yucatan. I've had a hunger to visit those parts for a long time, and that would be as good a spot as any to hole up until the trails grow cold. I could come back up here in four or five years as a Señor Lopez, trader in vanilla beans and peppers."

Cora felt an ache rise in her as Bones spoke of a fairly quick departure from her realm of New Orleans. Her bare forearm unconsciously rose and pressed her breasts hard.

"Bones, something else I been meaning to ask you."

"Sure, shoot away."

"How do you reckon things got as bad as they were down on that farm? I did some time here in Louisiana, and they work you plenty hard, but that was a mean piece of shit running the show down there at Sugarland."

"You aint wrong there. I can't put my finger on it completely. It has something to do with the failed glory of Texas, the fact that she never was quite what she could have been and claimed to have been. That's why they seem to make such a conscious effort—the warden and the bulls—towards refining the intensity of their cruelty until it's like a sharply honed Bowie knife that cuts right to the bone. They don't put up for no shit, no sir. Which is okay. But the other end of that, that failure of pride, which makes them treat the prisoners as being too low to lick the shit off their boots, that's wrong."

"You're damned straight about that." That's the damndest wrong I've ever seen. Say, what ever become of that Barnes boy you took a liking to, that bull rider."

"He got paroled. Right in the middle of cotton picking, too."

"He did!"

"Yep. His mama had a bee in her bonnet and she turned loose that bee on the judge that sent her son up. I was glad to see him get out before I played old Billy Hell with that cotton wagon. I dropped him a letter the other day. There was something about him that reminded me strongly of myself at that age. I wanted to spare him a few of the windrows I had to hop."

Benna reached over and lit up one of Connors' cigars. At Bones' surprise, she remarked, "Can't let him have all the fun. Besides, it's *fine* tobacco."

"That it is. And you are gettin' saucy. What say we go make those bedsprings sing and leave Bones a chance to make up to Cora Lee."

"Umm. I'm ready."

As they got up to leave, Connors turned to Cora and said, "That's y'all's bed in yonder and it's a lot softer than this here kitchen table."

Cora for once had no reply. She lowered her eyes and smiled.

Connors spoke to Bones once more, "See you in the mornin'. We got lots more talkin' to do. I just might help you get to Yucatan with a little bitty loan, which of course, you'll have to repay in person when the note runs out."

"Sounds just like prison."

And Connors smiled widely again, the smile speaking from years of unspoken meaning carried by that one gesture.

When they were gone, it was Cora's turn to blush. "Well, would you like to go, hmm, in yonder?"

"Yes."

"Yes, what?"

"Yes, I'd like to."

"Yes, let's."

* * *

When they entered the bedroom with a big four poster bed in the middle, Cora, still somewhat shy, slid around to the other side of the bed. When she saw him unselfconsciously strip off his plain khakis, she turned to face him as she undressed. She undid the buttons quickly down the front of the white dress, her flesh gleaming like freshwater gold in the light from the yellow lamp. She hesitated. Bones reached for the cord. "No, leave the light on." He turned and looked at her. The pupils of her eyes were deep pools of liquid firelight. Bones' heart felt like smoke. Her panties and brassiere slipped away like a rubber band snapping, and she knelt on the bed naked, her back straight, in wait for him. Bones, stunned by her beauty, filled his eyes. She was all of flesh that flesh could want of flesh.

Her nipples, the thickness and color of ripe plums, rose like small breasts on top of her breasts. Her lips opened to meet his. At the last, his eyes sought hers; his spirit as thirsty as his flesh. Her breasts swelled in the cup of his palms.

Bones knew he was rusty, but knew too that it didn't matter with her, and didn't matter with him either. The candle burned but a few moments, then burst into soaring flame, and hot wax and oil flowed down the smooth muscles of the twined thighs.

After, Bones lay with his head between Cora's breasts, his mouth and hands giving and taking pleasure from her firm velvet-skinned nipples. When he tried to speak, the words caught in his throat, and a few tears welled in his eyes instead and trickled down between her golden breasts. Cora was full in her heart, too, and said nothing for a long while. Other men had given her pleasure; none had ever given her this ache, this mystery of awareness of being more than she had been before.

"Do you think about it much, Bill? Those days and weeks and years in prison."

Bones could speak now. "Not much. Less and less after today. Some last dam broke loose. I used to think about it though, and mostly it was not about what it was like. I'd think instead of all the men I knew still locked up in that hell, and a cold burst of shame would wash over me. At times like that, I think I'd go and cut my throat in the town square if it'd do any good."

"Hush. Hush. I'll never let you do that. Not here in my New Orleans. Not here in my Louisiana." Then neither spoke for awhile, but simply moved with and for each other.

"If you go to Yucatan, I'm coming with you."

Bones meant to say *I would love to have you along,* but sleep was seeping through his limbs, and he merely said, "I would love you. . . ."

She cradled his head in her smooth arms. "Yes. In the morning, we'll talk about Yucatan."

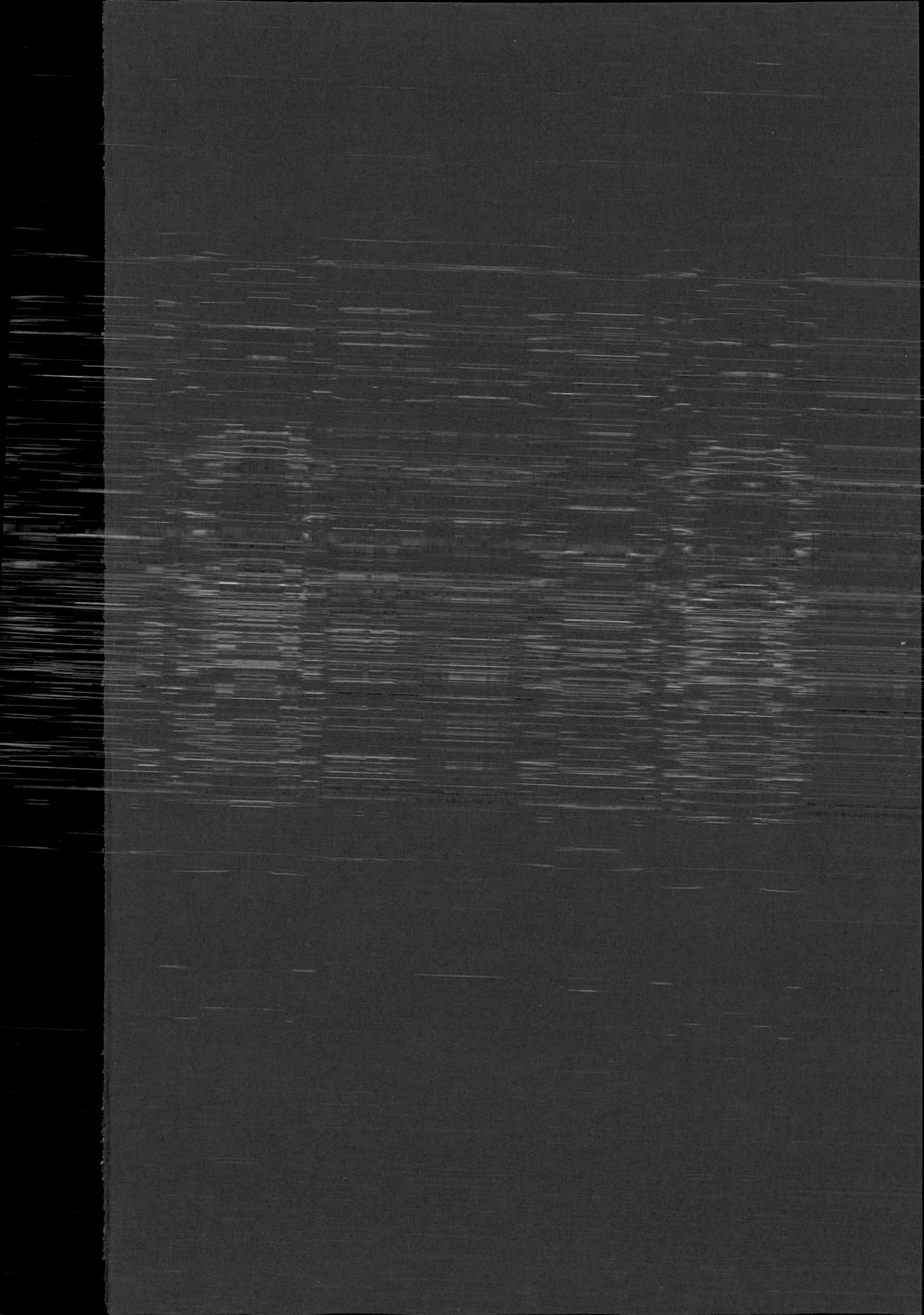